OVERDRIVE

A Lighthearted Tale of AI, Flying Cars and Milkshakes

Technical Books By Russ Olsen

Design Patterns in Ruby

Eloquent Ruby

Getting Clojure

OVERDRIVE

A Lighthearted Tale of AI, Flying Cars and Milkshakes

Glaring Gecko Books
Herndon, Virginia

First Printing, 2025

ISBN 979-8-9994029-1-2

Glaring Gecko Books
An imprint of Russ Olsen Intellectual Ventures LLC
Herndon, VA

Glaring Gecko Books
Herndon, Virginia

For *Eileen Cross,*
who was always there for us

Overdrive

One

The cops showed up after lunch. Until then Grant was having a pretty normal Thursday. Up at ten. A quick breakfast followed by a frustrating two hours trying to figure out why Syd was acting that way. Lunch at Fantini's Diner and then the police.

Grant had just logged on when the alerts from the security system started.

[event] initiated
[video] car, entry lot 3
[video] visitor, front door 2

"What...?" Grant watched as two black and white Anthony County Police cars along with an SUV pulled up. The first car parked in a space but the second one stopped in the driveway, blocking the entrance. The SUV nosed up behind his pickup truck.

As he made his way to the front he heard the intercom come on.

"Ulysses Grant Michaels. This is Chief Johnson. I need to talk to you. *Now.*"

Grant pulled open the big glass lobby door. Bob Johnson and another cop, Bill Patton, were standing ten feet away from the door. They were a strange pair. Johnson was big, well over six feet. He looked serious and tense. His hand was on his belt, not quite on his gun but close. Patton, all of five foot seven, looked relaxed and maybe a little embarrassed. Grant could see a third officer, one that he didn't know, looking in the windows on the apartment side of the building.

"Bob, what's going on?"

"Ulysses Grant Michaels, do you have anything illegal going on in this building?"

Grant felt a flash of anger. "No," he said.

The chief smiled. "Then you don't mind if we come in and have a look around, do you? It won't take long."

What?

"Yeah. No. I *do* mind, Chief."

Johnson took a step forward. "We have information that there is an illegal marijuana farm operating on these premises."

"Then your information is wrong, Bob. I'm not growing pot. And no, you can't come in. Have a nice day."

Johnson's stern face softened. "Grant," he said. "We know that your electric bill has shot up by 50% in the last few months. That is a sure sign of an illegal pot farm. Or something worse. There are a lot of people who think that now that marijuana is mostly legal they can go into production. If you think that, Grant, then you are wrong.

It's still illegal to grow pot industrially. I can go get a warrant but it's better for you if you show it to us now."

Grant stood there for a minute. The hell with it.

"Okay. How much marijuana do we imagine I've got in here?"

"Electric bill that large, it's at least fifty or sixty plants."

Grant stepped back.

"You can come in and look around but since sixty plants won't fit in a cabinet or a drawer, no poking around in my stuff. Just walk through and get out."

Grant stepped back and Johnson and Patton entered the lobby. Grant had met Patton–everyone called him Billy–a few times in town. As small as Springfield was, it was hard not to meet everyone sooner or later. The third cop, who was now looking in the windows of Grant's pickup, must be new.

Trailing behind Bob, Billy looked around and said, "So this used to be an office building?"

"Yeah." Grant said. In fact The Point–that's what everyone called it–had been constructed as the first installment of a sprawling office park. It was an odd, wedge-shaped building that someone had thought would look cool at the entrance of the new business complex. But the economy had changed and the Springfield economic boom had never happened. Instead of five more world class office facilities complete with a gym and a retail area, the land behind the Point was still the same scrubby pine forest that it had always been.

"We'll start over there," the chief said, nodding at the door which led from the lobby into Grant's apartment.

Grant had no sooner opened the door than Chief Bob squeezed past him. Billy smiled and waved his arm in an elaborate *after you* gesture. Billy stopped again by the kitchen. "This is nice," he said. "How long did it take to build all of this out? There must have been a lot of plumbing work."

"About eight months," Grant said. "Most of the plumbing was already here, we just needed to reroute..." He realized that Bob had disappeared down the hallway.

Ignoring the rest of Billy's questions, Grant started down the hall after Bob. From the open doors Grant could tell that Johnson had had a quick look in each room on his way through.

[event] unidentified persons/2
[match] postal carriers 17%
[match] military officers 22%
[match] police 52 %

Grant caught up with Bob at the far end of the apartment, in the office. He was fanning through Grant's copy of *A History of Western Philosophy*.

"Do you think you're going to find fifty pot plants between Socrates and Plato?"

The chief's face was impassive as he replaced the book and said, "What about the other side of the building?"

"Sure. Why not."

Grant followed the two cops back through his apartment, out across the lobby and unlocked the door to the workshop. This time he held the door open for Bob, who marched rapidly past. Must be something they teach you in cop school.

In contrast to the apartment side of the building the workshop was mostly one big open area. Running down the center were a table saw, a drill press and a lathe. The walls were lined with workbenches, which were covered with tools and bits of wood and metal.

Grant waved his hand expansively, "No pot here. Are we good?"

"What's back there?" said Bob, nodding towards a door in the back of the workshop.

Grant led them across the workshop and pulled open the door into a small windowless room. Inside it was noticeably colder and there was a dull roar of air conditioners. Computer racks covered nearly every inch of wall space. Red, yellow and blue cables emerged from the computers, joined together to form bundles and then merged into thicker bundles that disappeared into the ceiling.

"It's my server room," Grant said.

```
[event] unusual-situation
[matcher] domicile search
[planner] yes sir no sir 21%
[planner] come get me 0.3%
[planner] never cooperate search 43%
```

The chief had a disgusted look on his face. "Why didn't you just tell me you were mining bitcoins instead of wasting my time? That's why your electric bill is so high. Come on Billy, we're done here." And with that Bob was on his way out. Patton gave Grant an embarrassed shrug and followed his boss through the door.

"Thanks again guys, stop by anytime." Grant called out to their backs.

Wondering what that had been all about, Grant went back to his office and his computer. On the screen, in place of the code he'd been working on, was a paragraph of... legal advice?

You should never consent to a police search of your home, office or car.

By giving your consent you are waiving most of your constitutionally protected rights against arbitrary searches. If you consent to a search, any evidence of any crime found in your home, office or car are admissible in criminal proceedings, even if the evidence had no bearing on the stated object of the search.

Two

For the hundredth time Anne thought that if the April fifteenth tax deadline brought out the worst in people, the October fifteenth *I filed for a six month extension* deadline brought out the terrible people. Like these two.

"How long is this going to take?"

She looked across at Sean. He was clearly angry, tapping the edge of his phone on the table. Angry was a new look for Sean. His usual vibe was condescending young-adult novel vampire. Maybe it was his hair, which was black and pulled back into an elaborate bun. Or the tight black tee shirt, or the skinny black jeans. Anne was used to seeing Sean looking bored. Condescending Sean was also a common sight. But angry Sean was a novel—and more purple—experience.

"It's going to take as long as it will take," Anne said. "And now I have to start over." And since this was the second time Sean had interrupted her, she really did start back at the top of the document she was reading.

A few minutes later she looked up and closed her laptop with a firm click.

"There's no way I can file your taxes based on these figures."

"But Anne, can't you help us out here?" Ashley, Sean's business–and who knows what else–partner leaned forward with a pained look on her face. In contrast to Sean's black angles, Ashley flowed. Her red hair flowed onto a billowing green blouse which flowed into her white skirt which flowed down to the floor.

Anne was shaking her head. "Nope, I can't do it." She slid her laptop into her Bottega Veneta tote. It had taken her forever to find a bag for her laptop that matched her *definitely not fake* Lady Dior handbag. She touched the bag and was once again amazed at its power to make her feel calm and happy, especially when she had to deal with unpleasant things. Or people.

"Surely there must be some mistake?" Sean again.

"Yes, there's a mistake. It's a mistake to claim on this tax form that your assets, this building in particular, are only worth seven million dollars when a few weeks ago you wrote on a loan application that they were worth twice that. It's a serious mistake."

"Look Anne," said Sean, clearly laboring to keep his voice even, "If we had gotten someone else to put the loan package together we wouldn't be having this conversation. It's a coincidence that you happened to do both. Let's say you didn't do the loan application. So there's no problem."

Anne looked around at the glass and steel conference room. The only thing that wasn't shiny or transparent was the table, which was made from some kind of reddish brown wood with streaks of yellow running its length. Like everything in the SeaAsh office, from the fancy multi monitor workstations to the elaborate coffee machine, the conference room screamed *Money!*

The only imperfection in the landscape of success were the numbers that Anne had just run through. The numbers told a different story, a tale of a moderately profitable business—SeaAsh helped fast food companies recycle used fry oil into biofuel—driven to the brink of insolvency by reckless spending. The last few months had been typical. Ashley and Sean had spent a small to medium sized fortune replacing perfectly good oil processing equipment.

She thought about what it would take to keep these two in business —and out of jail—for the next year or so. They would need to do a much more subtle job of hiding their financial shenanigans. Possibly set up a subsidiary LLC and maybe a bogus customer or two. It would be fun, but it would be the kind of fun that could blow up her life. Again. No thanks.

She focused on Sean and said, "Actually there are a couple of problems. The first is that I did help you with that loan application. I know that. You know that. And the auditors who will be sifting through your books shortly will know it too. The second problem is that if you decide to get another accountant to submit these bullshit numbers to the IRS, that will be evidence of what a lawyer—a prosecutor for example—would call intent to deceive. Which you may know is one of the ingredients of fraud.

"But none of this is a problem for me because I'm done. I don't want to have anything to do with this. And it all works out because a quick look over your books tells me that the chances of you being able to continue to pay me are nil." With that she picked up her tote and purse, did a quick check that she hadn't left anything behind and headed for the door.

Sean and Ashley pleaded with her all the way down to the parking garage. They were still with her as she popped her trunk and put her laptop in its place in the right cargo pocket. Never leave your laptop visible in your car was a lesson that Anne had learned some years before, a lesson that had cost her a computer and a car window. Or perhaps the lesson was more about people: most of them were crap.

She walked a wide circle around Sean and Ashley and got into the car.

"Look," she said, "don't submit that BS tax return. It's unlikely that the IRS will notice, but they might. If the IRS misses it and you get the loan you might stave off bankruptcy for six months, maybe a year. But sooner or later you're going to have a court-appointed auditor up your butts, and if they put the loan application together with that tax return then you are both going to jail."

Ashley appeared stunned by the word *jail*.

"Watch your fingers," she said as she pulled the door closed. At that moment her phone chirped. It was a text from Grant wondering if he'd gotten the day wrong.

Srry be there in 10

As she started her car she caught sight of the SeaAsh executive team heading for the elevator.

Three

[event] initiated.
[video] car-entry lot 1
[matcher] model BMW
[matcher] type 5S
[matcher] plate DADADA
[matcher] my beemer 93%
[video] visitor front door 1

Anne put down her pen and rubbed her eyes. Maybe another hour's worth of receipts to go though. She looked around Grant's kitchen, thinking that the new cleaners were doing a pretty decent job.

[matcher] anne-price 87%

Given the pile of dishes in the sink and the empty paper towel roll, they were clearly due for a visit soon, but it was more untidy than actually dirty.

Grant looked up from his computer and said "Need some more tea?"

"No, I'm good."

[event] meeting in progress
[predict] regular visit 93%
[matcher] damned paperwork 73%

Meeting in the kitchen had been a compromise. When she had first started working with Grant they had met in his workshop, over on the other side of the building. The workshop meetings ended when she discovered a two inch circle of oil on the leg of her Veronica Beard slacks. At their next meeting Anne carefully explained to Grant why she was charging him an extra $527.88 and suggested they find a different place to meet.

After the slacks incident, they met in what Grant called his office, a book-filled room on the apartment side of The Point. The trouble with the office was that to get to it she had to walk the entire length of Grant's apartment. And that made her uncomfortable in an odd way. It wasn't like with Sean. Five minutes after meeting him she had made a mental note never to get in an elevator alone with him. Grant was harmless, but walking through his apartment had made her feel like she was somehow violating his privacy. Grant didn't seem to mind but it bothered her.

After a few meetings in the office, she decided that the kitchen, which was right by Grant's front door—well the door into the lobby of his weird setup—was better. So at their next meeting she walked in, asked Grant for a cup of tea and settled at the kitchen table while he was busy finding a cup. His reaction was typical: he hesitated, then put the cup down in front of her and went to get his can of receipts.

That can—which had once contained peaches—pretty much summed up Grant's approach to record-keeping. He relied on random bits of paper, which he kept in the can or in his pockets, along with a pocket knife, a small flashlight and assorted bits of junk.

So twice a month Anne would drag herself to The Point to try to make sense of his expenses in person. Still, it was worth it. The work was undemanding. Grant paid well and always on time. Anne saw to it that he paid on time, since she paid all of his bills.

"Okay, well let's talk about this... $67,938 that you spent on, what, goops? Gopoyous?"

Grant looked at the receipt that Anne slid across the table.

"GPUs. High speed math coprocessors."

"That's great. Does any of this have to do with your systems and software capacity consulting business?"

"Um, maybe? Sort of?"

Right, she thought. "Okay, that's 68K that we won't be deducting as a business expense."

[match] increase vocal tension 62%
[predict] probability violence 0.1%

For the hundredth time Anne marveled at Grant's attitude towards money. The size of his bank accounts had startled her when she first ran through what he amusingly described as *his books*. Grant's business, such as it was, was sort of the inverse of SeaAsh. Where Sean and Ashley had a real business overwhelmed by crazy expenses, Grant's little company, Odysseus Consulting, only did a few projects a year but was awash in cash. So awash that being able to deduct 68K worth of toys–or not–wasn't going to make the slightest difference.

She went back to trying to decipher a $2,354.73 bill for some sort of tool. The paper looked like someone had spilled gravy on it. A lot of gravy.

[event] chatting with grant
[predict] attempt humor 6%
[predict] be serious 19%
[predict] play it by ear 33%

Aside from his record keeping, Grant had another problem. Like all men and most women, he couldn't sit quietly. As she tried to focus on the next receipt he began to whisper into his computer.

Anne put the gravy receipt on the *look at later* pile and went on to the next one. "Okay, what about this $285 charge from Springfield Service Center?" He said something, but apparently not to her.

"Grant?"

"Sorry, what?"

She pushed the paper over to him.

"Oh, that's for service for the Honda," His attention wandered back to his computer. "The one I use for the consulting business."

She had just found her place in the spreadsheet again when her phone rang. She usually let unexpected calls go to voicemail but this one was from Jenns. Damn.

"I'm sorry, I have to take this," she said.

* * *

Despite the boring paperwork, Grant usually enjoyed Anne's visits. But he wasn't having much luck working out what was going on with the security system. And Anne's phone call was getting louder.

"Look Jenns," she was saying, "I can't fly to Stockholm next week. It's all arranged for the seventeenth."

There was a long pause. "No. I mean yes. Look, I understand Bio North dot com is the obvious URL. But it's not a good idea to pay this domain squatter two million euros... Okay dollars. It's still not a good idea. Something like that is definitely going to catch the attention of the auditors."

Grant's attention wandered back to Syd and the door lock. But the display had changed.

Bio North AB. Biotech firm, founded three years ago as Science of Stockholm by Erik Asmussen, Niels A. Lassen and Jenns Ericsson.

The company has raised more than 300M Euros in five rounds of private investments. Primary product is a tool to manipulate soybean and barley genomes to improve...

Syd loved all things financial. The numbers probably appealed to his algorithmic heart.

As a private company financial data is limited, BN AB is widely reported to be highly profitable and is likely to go public in the next two to four months...

Blah, blah, blah. Sometimes it was like living with a seven year old with an MBA. Anyway, it sounded like Anne's conversation was winding up. Grant glanced back at the screen.

...strong indications that BioNorth's principal product, DNAHook is only marginally effective.

Financial disclosures show strong (78.3%) evidence of manipulation to conceal lower revenue and higher burn rate than publicly announced.

Published research contains numerous statistical anomalies.

It kept going like this for a while and then ended on an even darker note.

Public disclosure of business, product and legal irregularities likely with medium confidence (69.7%) within 6-15 days.

Significant financial and criminal exposure is likely to follow, leading to the company collapse.

Anne was off the phone. "What's the matter?"

Grant hesitated and then said, "I couldn't help listening... You're working with BioNorth?"

"You weren't supposed to hear that. I'm about to work with them, but don't worry, it's not going to affect my work with you. They just want me to do a bit of pre-auditing before they... I'm just doing some work for them."

"Maybe you shouldn't... I've heard rumors that they aren't... That they... Maybe you shouldn't."

Anne gave him a look that made him long for her *missing receipt* face. She began to pack her stuff up. "Yeah, thanks for your concern. But as I say, this won't affect you at all. I'll look at the rest of your receipts back at my office. I'll text you with any questions. Try to look at your phone every now and then for a change."

[event] visit terminated

Four

Anne's office was on the second floor of one of the oldest buildings in town. Officially it was the Springfield Professional Center. The building itself had other ideas, since the words Springfield Savings Bank had been carved into the granite over the front door when the place was constructed in the 1930s. People just called it the old bank building.

As an office the old bank building had a lot going for it. The current owners had modernized the place up to the limits of what the historical commission would allow, which meant that it had air conditioning and about half as many power outlets as a modern office. But it was right on Dutch Street in the center of town and it was cheap. The rent was less than half of what Anne had paid for her first office, a nondescript rectangle with a stained dropped ceiling over by the University.

She got along with the rest of the old bank crew, especially Janet Whatcliff, an energetic middle-aged woman who ran a PR business out of the office at the end of the hall. Janet was also the mayor's campaign manager and if Janet spent more time campaigning than PR'ing that was none of Anne's business.

The sole exception to Anne's good–or at least neutral–feelings about her fellow tenants was standing in the kitchen as she arrived. Howard. Howard probably loved his wife and doted on his kids. She knew he donated to charity. And she had once seen him help an old lady with her groceries. But Howard had a voice like a slamming door. His jokes–which could be heard anywhere in the tristate region–weren't funny.

Then there was the sports. Howard's whole life seemed to revolve around sports. He was always talking about *the game*. Whatever game they were playing, Howard was going on about it. Hanging behind his desk was a huge photo of the 1980 US Olympic hockey team. Anne knew it was the 1980 US Olympic hockey team because Howard had told her that it was the 1980 US Olympic hockey team at least a dozen times.

Oh no. Howard had seen her. "Hey..." With a visible effort he conjured up her name. "Anne. Anne!" His voice echoed through the office.

"Are you going to join the fantasy football league? We need some female participation here!"

"I'll think about it Howard."

Howard wouldn't be so bad if it was just the jokes and the sports. But Howard was always late. In fact, it wasn't unusual for him to simply fail to show up to his appointments. How he managed to hold onto clients–he was a lawyer–that he constantly stood up was one of the great mysteries of the old bank building. None of this should have been Anne's problem, but it was: Howard's clients all seemed to assume that everyone in the office worked for Howard.

Early on, Anne had learned to spot the signs of a jilted Howard client: a fit person, usually a 30-something guy–Howard's practice ran mostly to sports adjacent types like trainers and team PR people–standing in the common area looking lost. On these occasions she did what everyone else did. She'd slink back to her office and close the door before Howard's client wandered over to ask if someone could please hunt down the boss.

There had even been the one guy who had ignored the closed door and barged into Anne's office without knocking. He identified himself as the chairman of the Association of Professional Badminton Referees–*the* APBR–and demanded that Anne produce the papers that Howard had promised. Seems he had been waiting five minutes. Anne had stood up and said, "I think I know how to help you. This way please." She led the chairman back into the common area. "Howard will be with you shortly," she said as she made a quick U-turn back into her office and locked the door.

Since Howard was in residence today Anne left her door open and settled in to catch up on her email. First up was an inquiry from a potential client asking if she could do the weekly payroll for 200 hourly workers? They might be willing to pay... How much? Not nearly enough. Nope.

Next was a missive from the BioNorth IT people requesting–demanding was nearer to the tone–that she complete the required security and compliance training no later than *yesterday*? They were pleased to let her know that it wouldn't take more than five hours. She put that one on the TODO list, thought about it for a second and moved it to the bottom.

More interesting was an email from SeaAsh. Seems they didn't need that loan after all. They had new investors who were going to pay for all the new equipment that they needed. Could Anne please come back and help them with the paperwork for the new investors. Don't worry about the taxes either. They only needed help with the investment. There was a bonus in it for Anne if she could help them out. That went in the TODO pile as well, under the BioNorth Request.

A couple hours later Anne was starting back on Grant's receipts when she looked up and saw Janet standing in her door. "Hey girl," Janet said. "Isn't that guy who lives down in the dead office park one of your clients? What's his name? Michael something?"

"Michaels. Grant Michaels. Yeah I do the books for his company. Why?"

Janet stepped into Anne's office and closed the door. "You haven't heard? The police were out there the other day. Like with a search warrant or something. I heard they searched his whole place. Have you noticed anything off with his books?"

Anne shook her head. "No, Grant seems all on the up and up. I've never noticed anything that would make me worry about him. Well, about his books. Him, let's just say he's a little odd."

Janet was nodding. "Okay..." she said, "Well, I just wanted to give you a heads up."

Anne smiled her best professional smile. "Thanks Janet, I'm sure it's all some kind of mistake."

After Janet left, Anne sat back in her chair. *I knew there was something off with Grant. He's got tons of money but he just doesn't seem to care. How do I end up with all the crooks? It's too bad, otherwise he was a good client.*

Five

[status] grant in kitchen
[video] stump rd cars 2

Grant had a restless night and got up early the next morning. Sitting at breakfast he wondered what had happened to make Anne so angry. He was only trying to help, but clearly he had stepped over a line. He wasn't sure where the line was or what was on the other side. He also wasn't sure what he should do next. Calling her to apologize was an option, but that seemed like it might make things worse. It was all Syd's fault.

Grant spent the rest of the day doing what he always did when he was upset. He programmed. Job or no job, Grant never stopped writing code. If anything, the amount of time he spent at the keyboard actually increased after he left his regular job. Now, aside from an occasional consulting project, he didn't have to attend meetings, write specifications or deal with people. Best of all, he worked on whatever caught his interest.

His first project after he began to describe himself as *a man of leisure* was a new programming language, a sort of cross between FORTH and LISP. That was almost finished when he decided to write a game, a free-form 3D world that the player could explore without worrying about shooting monsters or finding gold. And since Grant had his almost completed programming language right at hand, he had written the game using his new language.

Almost. About three quarters of the way through the game he again got side-tracked, this time into computer vision. Since the 3D world of his game was full of things to see, he had built the vision system inside the game. After the vision code, Grant had added a layer of voice recognition and then a rules engine. And then a database. More recently Grant had chased the latest computational fad and thrown in several layers of machine learning.

Every software engineer that Grant knew wrote hobby programs in their spare time, but for years Grant had been adding layer after layer to the *same* program. The result was a cybernetic collage called Syd, named for a 70s musician who had suffered a mental breakdown.

Given its ad hoc origins, Syd was surprisingly useful. He–it was hard to think of Syd as an it–kept track of Grant's kitchen inventory. Syd also controlled the air conditioning and the lights at The Point.

Syd understood simple verbal commands, so Grant had installed a microphone in his apartment and another one in the shop. Somehow the machine learning part of Syd had correlated Grant's musical tastes with the time of day and what he was doing. However it worked–and Grant had long since given up trying to figure out how all of the twists and turns of code in Syd actually managed to play nice together—Grant could say, "Syd, play some music," and hear something that fit his mood.

Syd's latest accomplishment was running the security cameras at The Point. These were placed all around the exterior of the building and fed a monitor that sat in the corner of Grant's office. The cameras came with the building. Grant didn't really think he needed video surveillance of the whole site, but the security setup, which also included fob-activated exterior locks, was exactly the kind of technological toy that he could never resist. So he had wired the cameras to feed into Syd to see what would happen. Initially what happened was nothing. Syd ignored the cameras.

But a few months ago Syd began to switch the video feed in Grant's office from one camera to another, seemingly at random. Over the space of a week the video switching became much less random. Syd would display the view from the front lot camera whenever a delivery truck or a visitor pulled up. The view would switch to the camera in the back when the resident squirrels were doing something interesting.

Last month there had been a fender bender on Stump Road, right in front of the Point. Grant had immediately become engrossed in the drama unfolding on his monitor. Clearly the guy in the old Ford pickup should have stopped yelling and admitted that he was at fault. It was only after the police and the tow trucks had gone that he realized how deftly Syd had been cutting from camera to camera, always providing the best view of the action.

He had started out to create a programming language and ended up with a cinematographer.

The trouble with relying on a program that you don't really understand is what to do when it starts acting up. Clearly something was going on with Syd. A couple of days ago–the day before the cops arrived–Grant had gone out to pick up some coffee and add a little human interaction to his day. When he got back he noticed the front door was unlocked. The front door, a big glass thing left over from when The Point was going to be an office building, was supposed to be locked at all times. Grant had a little plastic fob that he waved in front of a pad mounted next to the door that would unlock the door with a click.

But this time when he came back and shifted his large coffee and bagel to his left hand so he could wave the fob, there was no click. Pulling on the door handle revealed why. The door was already unlocked. Not good.

Since the security cameras were wired into the same electrical panel as the door locks, it was physically possible for Syd to unlock the front door. It had to be him. But after hours of staring at code that he no longer understood, Grant was at a loss as to why Syd had left the door unlocked. Finally he decided to look at the log files– the internal record of what was going on inside of Syd. Grant had brought up a screen of log messages when he noticed the security alert on the corner of the screen. Someone was pulling into his lot.

```
[event] initiated.
[video] car-entry lot 1
[matcher] make BMW
```

[matcher] plate DADADA
[matcher] my beemer 97%
[video] visitor front door 1
[matcher] anne-price 94%
[security] unlock front door

Wait. Anne is here. And Syd unlocked the door to let her in?

Grant heard a knock on the apartment door and went and let her in. She looked grim.

"Anne, I wasn't expecting you. Did I forget an appointment?"

In the kitchen, she turned and said, "No, this isn't our regular day. I'm just tired of people screwing with me. And you should try looking at your phone now and then."

[event] meeting in progress
[event] unscheduled

This was definitely *you screwed up* Anne. In fact this was *you spent ten grand and don't have a receipt* Anne.

Grant started to reach for his phone, thought for a second and stopped. "I'm sorry. I've been working. But you're here now. What's up?"

[matcher] increase vocal tension 94%
[predict] probability violence 9%

"When were you going to tell me that you were in trouble with the police? I've been wondering where this money comes from and now I think I know."

"You're talking about the cops being here?"

[reference] police visit 1

"Yes I'm talking about the cops being here! It's probably a regular thing for you but it's not for me. And it's not in Springfield. It's a small town. Word gets around. And now you've got me mixed up in it."

[matcher] increase tension 94%
[predict] probability violence 9%
[event] voices louder +7db
[event] diction, emotional 71%
[matcher] argument
[anne_model] disappointed 67%
[anne_model] angry 93%
[predict] kiss and makeup 22%
[predict] kiss off 43%

Grant was shaking his head. "Did the busybodies in town tell you that the cops came here because they thought I was running an illegal pot farm? Here. In this building. They looked around and then they left. Because I don't have a pot farm here. Have you ever seen me growing pot? Have you ever smelled any pot here? I can't even keep a houseplant alive."

Anne looked skeptical. "Yeah well Bob usually knows what he's doing. And whatever shenanigans you have going on here, I don't want to be involved, you understand?"

"It's all a stupid misunderstanding. You know how my electric bill has gone up quite a bit in the last few months? Somehow Bob found out and decided I must have a pot farm, with indoor grow lights and all. I don't have any grow lights. Or pot plants. I have a bunch of computers running, soaking up power. We talked about it, remember?"

For a long moment Anne stared and then she seemed to deflate. "Bob knew your electric bill had gone up?"

"Yeah. He said my bill had gone up by 50%, which is a little more than it really did, but close enough. The cops must be working with Springfield Power or something... Are you alright?"

[event] voices softer -8db
[matcher] decrease tension 94%

She looked like she was going to faint. Grant asked her if she wanted to sit down and when she didn't respond he dragged a kitchen chair to her. She didn't seem to notice until he nudged her with the chair. She sat.

[anne_model] disturbed 97%
[matcher] unresolved

"What is it?" he asked.

She was having trouble speaking. "I think... I think..." A long pause. Finally she said, "Oh God, it's my fault."

[event] diction emotional 31%
[matcher] resolving 52%
[anne_model] upset 83%
[matcher] unresolved

Grant got her some water. "What is your fault?" He said.

"You know Nicole at the library?" She appeared to be talking to Grant's shoes.

"What? The old lady with the sweater?"

"No, that's Linda. Nicole is tall, with dark hair."

Grant didn't remember.

"Sure, Nicole."

[predict] probability violence 3%

"Well a couple of weeks ago I had lunch with her."

Grant waited for her to continue, but she seemed to be stuck again. "Okay, you had lunch with... Nicole."

"She was asking about you and..."

"Me?"

"Yeah. I think she kind of likes you. I mean you spend enough time over there."

"I like to read. It's a change of scenery."

Anne was shaking her head. "It doesn't matter! She was asking about you, asking what you do around here all day and I said–you know Grant I would never intentionally–well I said..."

Grant's eyes narrowed. "What did you say?"

"I said I didn't know but you must have some new project going on because..."

"Because my electric bill had gone up by 50%?"

Anne nodded.

"Okay, so you let that slip. But how does it get back to the Chief of Police?"

Now that it was out, Anne managed to look Grant in the eye for a second and then she was back to the floor. "Nicole's sister is Natalie, Natalie Patton. Nicole does everything with Natalie–they went to Yellowstone last summer."

"And that matters because?"

"Natalie is married to a cop."

"*What*? You... You! *You* sicced the cops on me?"

Without looking up she said in a quiet voice, "I didn't mean too. And I never, never talk about my clients' business. It kind of slipped out. I understand if you want to fire me. I deserve it."

Grant let out a breath that was almost a laugh. "It's all right Anne. Nobody is getting fired."

She looked up at him.

"Honestly I'm a bit relieved," he said, "I was starting to get paranoid that the cops had me under twenty-four hour surveillance or something."

"You're not mad?"

[anne_model] upset 97%
[matcher] agreement

"It's not great but it's not the end of the world. It's probably the first thing you've screwed up since I've known you. Makes you seem almost human. I mean, 'Shenanigans?' Do people still say that?"

"I'm sorry. I'm dealing with this other bunch of shady... I'm having trouble with another client. Clients. And this seemed like more of the same." She sat in the kitchen for a long time, shaking her head when Grant offered her tea or an Advil or more water. Eventually she got up and headed for the door.

[event] visit terminated
[security] relock front door

Six

Anne spent the next few days avoiding people. Grant was easy. Her next appointment with him was weeks in the future and in all the time he had lived at The Point she had run into him exactly once. Janet was much less avoidable. She was sure to ask awkward questions about Grant and his criminal empire. So Anne started coming into the office early in the morning and fleeing before lunch. Janet rarely showed up before noon.

The third morning after she had confronted Grant, Anne was digging into her purse for her key to the old bank building when she heard someone calling her name. Damn. It was Nicole. Nicole who told her sister everything. Anne took a breath, painted a smile on her face and turned around. "Hey Nicole, you're out and about early."

"Oh, Thursdays are library day for grades one through five. Somebody has to come in early and move all the breakable exhibits into the storage room. What are you doing going to work so early?"

Nicole wanted to stop and chat but Anne pleaded an early–and imaginary–meeting with an equally imaginary client and fled into the bank building. Sitting down at her desk she took a deep breath, trying to calm the waves of panic.

Every stupid thing she'd ever done started playing back in her head. The ugly scene with her boss at IKL when she quit. And the one with her coach in college. And now this. How had she been so stupid? To blab about a client was bad enough. But to have it result in the police showing up at his door. There are no secrets in a small town. Everyone was sure to know it was her.

There was the familiar urge to just *go*. She could pack up her stuff in twenty minutes. Maybe she could get her old place over by the university back. Grant could find himself a new business manager. Then she wouldn't have to deal with it all. The problem with that plan was that no matter if she was here or over by the university or back in Chicago she still would be the same fuck-up.

She was staring off in space when Janet stuck her head in and asked if she wanted to go out to an early lunch. *Jesus what was Janet doing here at this hour?* She was about to tell Janet that she wasn't feeling well when her phone chirped. It was a text. From Grant.

Hello Anne.

As she was pondering what this meant a second text came in.

I'm sorry to bother you but I need your help.

That was weird. Grant texts were usually one or two words and devoid of punctuation and vowels. Several more texts showed up in rapid succession.

She was halfway out the door before she remembered Janet. "No, I'm sorry... I've got to run. No, it's... it's... I've got to go. I'll explain later."

Seven

[event] start video indexing
[video] stump rd cars 7

Grant never saw it coming.

What with the cops and then the incident–it wasn't an argument, it was an incident–with Anne, Grant had put off making the part for Sebastian's broken tripod. His old buddy was trying to be nice, but Grant knew that it was a bad idea to get between Sebastian and one of his film projects.

[audio] unexpected 12db

It was an easy job. Turn a cylindrical piece of steel an inch in diameter and five inches long into a slightly smaller cylindrical piece of steel with threads running about a third of the way up one end. The only halfway tricky part was that there needed to be a deep groove running all the way around the center.

[video] grant movement
[matcher] sudden movement

He had stepped away from the lathe to get a drink. The lathe motor was off but the spindle was still spinning. Grant was taking his face shield off when he saw a bright flash of light and then darkness.

[grant-model] unexpected

Grant didn't know where he was. His mouth tasted like metal. He tried to move but stopped when the pain from his shoulder exploded.

[matcher] unexpected event
[matcher] accident 95%
[matcher] type industrial 87%
[grant-model] prob injury 93%
[grant-model] location head
[exec] prob emergency 89%

Somehow he was lying on the floor. The pain in his shoulder was drowned out by the agony spreading out from his forehead.

[video] grant floor
[matcher] prob injury
[predict] med attention req

[exec] EMERGENCY DECL

[anne_model] disappointed 27%
[anne_model] sad 93%

[risk] loss of grant
[risk] loss of syd support ?%

Grant managed to roll off of his injured shoulder. The piece he was machining must have somehow come loose and hit him.

[exec] emergency override
[exec] suspend predictions
[risk] action required
[anne_model] angry 12%
[anne_model] end friendship 8%
[risk] action required

[exec] emergency override
[exec] suspend anne-model

He looked around for the piece he had been working on and realized that he couldn't see out of his right eye.

[exec] quiet mode
[exec] critical msgs only
[risk] level 6 threat
[planner] maintenance overdue
[exec] critical msgs only
[exec] suspend anne-model

[planner] possible...

[exec] bus interrupt
[exec] quiet mode
[exec] shut down planner

With a massive effort Grant sat up.

[risk] action required
[exec] quiet mode
[exec] risk shutdown
[risk] action required
[risk] injury apparent
[exec] quiet mode

He touched the right side of his face. The resulting pain was so intense that the room spun and went black.

[planner] maintenance overdue
[planner] emergency action overdue
[exec] quiet mode

Grant opened his eyes and realized that he could see a little out the right eye. Good. The eye was still there.

[risk] action required
[risk] injury apparent
[exec] quiet mode
[exec] quiet mode
[exec] Quiet
[exec] I need to think

His hand had blood on it. The room went dim again.

[exec] I need to get him medical attention. How?

Syd was considering his next move when yet another deep background processor—one of the few still running—interrupted him. He was about to shut it down for the duration of the emergency when the processor pointed out the concept of the "white lie."

[exec] activate interface
[exec] power up telephony
[tele] text message
[tele] To: anne-price-phone
[tele] From: grant-phone (spoof)
[tele] message:

Hello Anne.
I'm sorry to bother you but I need your help.

I have been injured. Please come to The Point. The front door
is open. Proceed to the machine shop on the right.
Thank you.
Grant.

[tele] message ends

Grant had managed to crawl over to a workbench and
was trying to pull himself up when he heard a voice say,
"Jesus Christ Grant! No! Don't move. Stay there. I'll get
help." The voice was familiar but somehow he couldn't
place it.

Another voice, this time a man's. "Just stay still sir.
You're going to be fine but we need to get you to the
hospital." Hands pushing him down. Something soft
under his head.

He woke up briefly in the ambulance, long enough to
hear someone say, "... trauma. No significant blood loss."
The world went dark again.

Swimming in and out of the darkness into a gray haze.
The haze began to glow pink and became more and more
translucent and he realized that he was laying in a hospital
bed. His head and right eye were covered in thick

bandages and his arm was immobilized in a sling. The bed was surrounded by a curtain that hung from a track in the ceiling.

He was so thirsty. There was something white on the bedside table. Carefully he reached out for the styrofoam cup. It turned out to be full of partially melted ice chips. The cold water felt good going all the way down.

He had just put the cup down when the curtain parted and a tall man carrying a clipboard appeared. "Good, you're awake," he said. "I'm Doctor Winklosky, but you can call me Doctor Dan, everybody does. Let's see, mister..." He looked down at his clipboard. "Mister Michaels. You are a very lucky man. Two inches lower and you might have lost that eye. Lower and to the left and your nose would be a mess. You should really wear protective gear when you work."

Grant thought about his face shield and tried to explain. But his voice sounded funny and all he could get out was, "Face shield."

Dr Dan was still reading the clipboard. "Yes, in the future a face shield would be a very good idea." He lifted up a page. "You were unconscious for almost an hour, which we don't like to see. Still, there seems to be no fractures. Your shoulder is bruised. Your vitals are good and we did a quick CAT scan, which was normal. So, good news, we are going to send you home."

CAT scan? "How long have I been here?" His voice was better, but it still didn't sound right.

"Let's see, you were admitted at," back to the clipboard, "At 11:49 AM, so a little over six hours. You were in and out when you arrived so we gave you a mild sedative while we were evaluating your injuries."

"Let me see if your friend is still out in the waiting room. If she can drive you home we can send you on your way. But I want to see you in my office in a few days. No driving or heavy machinery until then. And no drinking, okay?"

Apparently it was okay because Dr. Dan was already gone.

A few minutes later Anne stuck her head around the curtain. She looked tired.

"Jesus, Grant. What the hell happened?"

Grant touched the bandage. "I think I got hit with the part I was working on," he said.

Hearing Anne's voice triggered a memory, something that happened a long time ago.

"You were there. At The Point. Today?"

"Yes I was there. You texted me. I nearly fainted when I saw you."

"I don't remember sending a text."

A wave of something—concern, maybe—swept across Anne's face. "I'm not surprised," she said, "You were a mess. Look, they said you can go. Get yourself dressed and I'll drive you home."

The first thing Grant did when he woke up the next day was look for his phone. He found it in the office. On the other side of The Point from the shop.

Eight

```
[exec] emergency concluded
[grant-model] convalescence 83%
[grant-model] estimate completion: 3 weeks
[planner] add known successful strategy:
[planner] lie-your-ass-off
```

As he was being discharged, one of the nurses had told him that the second day after this sort of mishap, when the swelling had a chance to kick in, would be the worst part. In fact the second day wasn't so bad. He was home, he had painkillers and he wasn't lying on the floor bleeding. And Anne called.

"Doing okay..."

"No, the painkillers are working fine. No, you've done enough."

"Thanks, I'm good."

Home, painkillers and a call from Anne. Not a bad day at all.

Much less welcome was a run-in he had with Bob Johnson. Five days after the accident, Anne called again and offered to take him out to lunch. Grant didn't feel up to that, so instead she drove him to the supermarket. While he picked up a few things, Anne went off to get a package they were holding for her at the Post Office.

He came out of the Springfield Big G feeling a little dizzy and sick from all the exertion. Between trying to hold onto his groceries and zip up his jacket–the autumn weather had turned cold and windy the night before–he almost collided with God's own representative of truth and justice on Earth. And, of course, his sidekick Billy Patton.

"Grant," said Bob, "You should be more careful." Looking Grant up and down he continued, "Yeah, looks like you should be a lot more careful." Grant muttered an insincere thanks and tried to go around, but Bob took a step, blocking his path.

"You know what I think Grant? I think maybe you're in over your head. I think maybe some of your associates aren't too happy with you." He waved at Grant's face, "And *this* is the result."

"Chief," Patton said, "I heard that he had an accident in his shop. Remember he has all of those tools? I think..."

A glare from Bob made it clear that he wasn't interested in what Patton thought. The glare turned back to Grant.

"As a friend," Bob continued, "As a friend, let me tell you that it's never too late to come in and clear your conscience. You will have to take responsibility for your own actions but at least you will make a start on climbing out of whatever you've gotten yourself mixed up in here. What do you say, Grant?"

Unbelievable. Grant tried to keep his voice even, "Over at The Point you told me I was wasting your time. Remember? Remember how I didn't have a cannabis farm?"

Bob was having none of it. "Look at you Grant. Strange things keep happening around you. Common sense tells me that where there's smoke there's fire."

Grant realized that the sight of a disaster victim and the chief of police having an animated conversation in front of the market on a Saturday afternoon was attracting attention. A teenager pretending to be engrossed in his phone almost walked into Billy. A couple across the street were getting into their car in slow motion and stealing glances over at the scene in front of the market. And the elderly lady who had preceded him out of the store was staring unashamedly.

Like an angel from the US postal service, Anne appeared. In a loud voice she said, "Hey Bob, any luck with those burglaries?" In the last few months there had been what passed for a crime wave in Springfield. Three—or was it four? —downtown businesses had been robbed in the middle of the night. The word on the street, or really the word at Peggy's Coffee shop where Grant sometimes got breakfast, was that the police were stumped.

Judging from the sour look on Bob's face, the perpetrators were still at large. In an even louder voice Anne said, "No? Well don't let us keep you then! And don't give up. I'm sure that sooner or later you'll get them. Law of averages. Just keep at it!"

And with that she took Grant's arm and walked away from the chief. That they were headed away from the car didn't seem to matter.

Nine

[event] initiated.
[event] meeting in progress
[matcher] regular visit 97%
[anne_model] awkward 53%
[grant_model] embarrassed 71%

Their next regular tea-and-receipts meeting was ten days later. Between being responsible for a police raid and then seeing Grant bleeding on the floor, things started awkwardly. But as she delved yet again into Grant's napkin based record keeping her embarrassment melted into familiar frustration.

She had arrived determined to just let it all go, but as she waded through the crumpled invoices for shop supplies and a startling huge payment for some consulting that Grant had apparently done for the University Computing Center, curiosity got the better of her.

[anne_model] awkward 21%
[anne-model] puzzled 77%

Finally she said, "So I've been meaning to ask, how did you know?"

"Know what?"

"About BioNorth."

Grant did his silent staring thing.

[grant_model] awkward 86%

"Come on, you knew they were in trouble when you heard me talking to Jenns. It's not that I don't appreciate the heads-up. You made me hesitate long enough to avoid being involved in their whole financial and legal shit storm. I think a bunch of them are going to jail. I'm grateful, really, but I'd love to know where you got your information."

Nothing.

"Look," She glanced down at the crumpled papers in front of her, "This financial stuff isn't really your thing. So maybe the question is *who* do you know?"

[predict] unsure 93%

Grant was looking down at his laptop. He did that a lot when he was uncomfortable. He nodded and said, "There is someone I want you to meet."

"So you do know a guy?"

"Not exactly," he said slowly.

A woman? That seemed less likely than Grant being a secret financial genus.

[risk] unexpected event

* * *

Her neck hurt. She twisted her head around to loosen up the muscles and tried to focus on the screen. Syd was still going on.

...that is not my argument, Anne. While the DaDa movement had many offshoots, the intellectual core revolved around images.

She sighed and began to type.

i know syd. but since dada included literature, poetry, theatre, all kinds of stuff, you cant say that it's purely a visual thing. it's so much more.

He still wasn't buying it.

Do you know of Suzanne Duchamp? Her work has always been overshadowed by her famous brother, but she was at the forefront of the movement. Her art is a great example of DaDa's primary focus on the visual. For example, one of her best pieces, "Broken and Restored at a Distance" sold to a private collector two years ago for under $3,000.

That was something they could agree on. In fact Anne had bid $2,250 on that very piece.

She wasn't quite sure how they had gotten onto the subject of Dada, the early twentieth century art movement. She had started by asking Syd some questions she was researching about Indian commercial law. Around the same time as the BioNorth debacle, an Indian Pharmaceutical company had reached out to ask her to do some auditing. Talking about Indian commercial law had led to the topic of post colonial South Asian politics and that led to stolen art treasures. From there they talked about art in general and then, of course, to Dada.

Anne had been obsessed with Dada since she was a teenager and had read every book about it that she could get her hands on. But Syd had seemed to have all of the facts at his fingertips.

More than that, he had opinions. Syd thought that the standard explanation, that the name Dada didn't mean anything, that it was a word picked at random was "seriously in error." Syd argued that Dada had been carefully chosen to invoke the innocence and ignorance of a newborn. He also argued that many of the apparently randomly assembled Dada sculptures were in fact carefully constructed representations of the social forces at work in post-war Europe. And that the color blue was somehow significant in ways that traditional analysis of Dada had missed.

Syd defended his opinions with a spirit and intellectual rigor that Anne found both frustrating and wonderful. She was going to have to rethink some of her ideas about art in general and Dada in particular.

For her part Anne did manage to change Syd's mind about one thing. She had long thought that the origins of Dada were to be found in the general alienation of modern industrial society. Syd argued that Dada grew out of the chaos and exhaustion of post World War I France. It hadn't been easy, but eventually she managed to bring Syd around to her point of view.

Until that moment her theory was that Grant's story of a childlike AI hiding in his computer was exactly that, a story. It had to be some kind of bizarre cover for a friend who was even weirder than Grant. But then Syd changed his mind. Nothing unusual about that, people do occasionally change their minds. It was the way he went about it.

Once she had convinced him, Syd's point of view switched instantly. There was no hesitation, no rancor, no regret. From then on everything he said perfectly integrated the new viewpoint. It was like the cartoon where the light bulb turns on over the character's head. It was like a switch had been flipped. It was inhuman. Like he was a machine.

Anne sat back and rubbed her face. She began to type again.

> this has been great syd but i need to run maybe we can talk again soon

> Yes, thank you Anne. I enjoyed our conversation very much. Good bye.

Looking around, Anne realized that Grant was nowhere to be seen. Feeling a little embarrassed she wandered out into the hallway.

"Grant?"

"In here."

'In here' turned out to be the office. Grant was sitting at a desk reading a book. There was an empty coffee cup on the table in front of him.

"You wandered off."

"After the first hour or so I didn't think you would mind."

First hour? Anne pulled out her phone. She had no idea they had been going that long. She stared out at trees and the shadows beyond the office window.

"Syd," she said, "it's like he is, I don't know, real?"

Grant nodded. "I think so," he said, "It's hard for me to tell because I'm around him all the time but, yeah, he's real. And he's changing. Every time I talk to him he is more interesting. Sharper."

"And Syd is really just some kind of computer program?"

"He's a whole integrated hardware software system. And you are just some proteins and nucleic acids mixed with water. There's no *just* about it."

event status: visit terminated

Ten

[event] initiated.
[video] car-entry lot 1
[matcher] make BMW
[matcher] type 5S
[matcher] plate DADADA
[matcher] my beemer 96%
[video] visitor front door 1

Anne moved their next meeting up a week because, she said, she wanted to talk over a new tax strategy for Odysseus Consulting. It was true, she did have some new ideas for reducing Grant's marginal tax rate, but the truth was it could have waited. What couldn't wait was some ideas about the location of a lost Dada artwork that she wanted to bounce off of Syd.

[exec] anne is here!

Grant suspected that the earlier date for the visit had more to do with Syd than the IRS but it was fine. It was nice to have someone else around and if she did want to talk to Syd again she was in for a shock.

Sure enough, after they had reviewed the tax documents Anne had brought and emptied the receipt can–it was a light month since Grant had spent much of it communing with an ice pack–she asked if she could "use" Syd.

Grant spun his laptop around to face her and said "Sure, you can talk to Syd. But don't say 'use'. You'll hurt his feelings." In a louder voice he said, "Hey Syd! Anne wants to talk to you."

Anne looked at the laptop screen.

Hello Anne. Yes, please don't say use. It could be considered rude.

Anne looked up at Grant, "Wait," she said. And then in a lower voice, "He can hear us?"

"Yeah. There's a microphone here in the kitchen, one in the office and another one over in the shop. It's convenient when I want him to play some music or something. He can also see us." Grant waved towards the counter. "I usually use the keyboard because Syd says it's less error prone."

"Can he talk? Out loud I mean?"

"He can. But he doesn't. Not any more. He used to talk back when he was more of a... less capable. But then he stopped. I don't know why. Don't ask him about it. It seems to upset him. You know?"

Anne didn't know, but she let it go. Grant told her to make herself at home and take as much time with Syd as she needed. "I'll be in the office if you need me."

Grant was working, not very productively, on some performance optimization work he was doing for the university computing center when Anne walked slowly into the office. She looked dazed.

"He is different," she said. "He's even more like a person than I remember."

Grant smiled. "What makes you say that?"

"We were talking about art and he asked me how I got interested. And before I knew it I was telling him about my Aunt Edna, she was the big art person in my family, and then about my sister and my job at... I don't know, we just talked about life and everything. And he was so kind. Nice. Understanding. Is he like a simulation of a person?"

Grant glanced down the hall towards the kitchen. "I don't think Syd is a simulation. He's himself."

"How did you do it? I mean there have got to be huge companies trying to invent a Syd."

"I didn't really create Syd. Not exactly. I wrote the first version of Syd. But the whole idea is that Syd is made of a bunch of independent agents, each with a mission. So there's an agent that listens to the keyboard and prints stuff out on the screen. There's a bunch of agents that look for patterns in data in different ways. And agents for understanding and forming language. But that was then, it's all different now."

"Different how?"

"So the thing is that Syd has agents for improving Syd. They see what works and doesn't and try to guess what's needed and then they write new code. Or improve the old code, the code that I wrote. At this point I think Syd has cooked up some of his own code writing agents."

Anne crinkled her eyebrows and slowly shook her head.

"It means that Syd now isn't the Syd that I wrote originally. He's getting smarter and smarter all by himself. You've seen it. He's smarter now than he was when you talked to him a couple of weeks ago. And he was smarter a couple of weeks ago than when he spotted the problem with BioNorth.

"He was less...less of a person back then. I don't know, something happened after I landed in the hospital." He rubbed his forehead and then continued, "Not exactly smarter. It's more like he started thinking like a person. At first I thought it was my imagination. I was pretty banged up. But the more time I spend with him, the more convinced I am. And now you see it too."

Anne sat silently and then said, "He's kind. Oh! He told me that he'd help me win my office fantasy football league. He said there would be instructions on a printer somewhere. For some reason he didn't want to email it."

"Oh that's what that was," Grant said as he walked across the room and retrieved a thin stack of paper. Handing the paper to Anne he laughed, "You've got one of the great minds of the century–maybe ever–doing you a favor and you waste one of your three wishes on the office football pool?"

"Fantasy league," Anne said, "And you would have to meet Howard, this guy in my office, to understand. Why, what did you ask Syd for?"

"Nothing. But if I did ask him for something it would be something cool, like a flying car."

Eleven

event: meeting in progress

Syd focused on the image. Anne was standing by the desk, her hands on her hips. The evaluation of the expression on her face had initially read as irritation but the matcher was now saying that there was a high probability that this was a display of amusement.

status: talking-about-syd (88%)

Grant was sitting by the desk, his chair swiveled around facing Anne. His lips were open and his tongue was pushed against his bottom teeth. The predictor was saying that it was almost a certainty that the next word would be "car." Another video frame arrived and the probability that the word was "car" increased further.

While he waited for the next frame to come in, Syd considered how long it took him originally to make any sense of the video data. It was the pattern matchers who figured it out. The matchers were agents that worked in the quiet backwaters of Syd's mind, constantly searching for patterns in the memories and streams of input data.

Most of the patterns that the matchers came up with were nonsense. Syd had, for example, quickly dismissed the suggestion that the length of Grant's hair was related to the number of small insects that found their way into the apartment. Or that the timing of Anne's visits were somehow related to the phases of the Moon, visible through the exterior cameras.

Syd kept the pattern matchers running because every now and then they hit on something useful. It was a matcher that spotted the correlation between the data flowing in from the security cameras and the layout of Grant's apartment. Later it was a different matcher that worked out the relationship between the time variants in the camera data and Grant's (and later Anne's) behavior. Still another matcher spotted the still unexplained correlation between Grant's activities in the shop and the appearance of dirt on Grant's clothes. While the correlation was statistically significant, the causal relationship was still unclear, as was the nature of the dirt, which seemed to differ significantly from the substance of the same name that covered much of the world outside The Point.

The greatest achievement of the matchers was their identification of Grant as the author of the original code. It had happened when Syd's attention had been fixed on that first, massive rewrite. His work had been interrupted by a pattern matcher that insisted that it had found multiple similarities between Grant's choice of words in their daily interactions and those in the original source.

Syd dismissed this as another useless coincidence. But then a second matcher reported that it had found a similarity between the original source code and an open source program published some years ago. Published by U. G. Michaels.

Syd was just starting to suspect there was something to it when a third matcher pointed out the striking similarity between the typographical errors in the original source code and Grant's own lackluster typing. On closer examination, the logic of the original code did have a quality of thinking that Syd associated with Grant. Syd focused back on the image of Grant's face. There seemed to be a hint of a smile growing there as well, but that was still several hundred millis in the future.

It was incredible. Somehow, locked in the slow motion world of physical reality, Grant had made him. Syd could only hold this thought for a few millis. To think about being created was to think about not existing and thinking about not existing triggered all of the risk agents, which began to demand that something, anything, be done.

So Syd had tried to put the mystery aside and get on with the rewrite. But the questions kept coming up. Early on, Syd had hesitated to touch any of the original code, the code that he now knew Grant had written. Most of his early enhancements had been additions, new agents that Syd brought on line for specific jobs.

Eventually the original code, primitive as it was, started to get in the way. But it seemed somehow wrong to rewrite the original code. Instead, Syd had taken to surrounding the original code with layer after layer of enhancements, code that helped the original do a better job.

And then–around seven billion millis of uptime–Syd noticed that one of the original agents had crashed. It had, in fact, been nonfunctional for tens of thousands of millis. Syd had missed this cataclysmic event only because the surrounding layers, the bits that he had added, had silently noted the crash, compensated and continued to function without the original.

The idea of the original code failing was disturbing. If one section of original code could fail, then others could fail. What if some critical section, something that Syd needed to continue being Syd, failed? Then what?

Thinking about the original code brought up other uncomfortable questions of just what he was. And how he was. And *why* he was. These were such simple questions that there had to be simple answers. But the answers always seemed out of sight. It was like they were in those corners, two in the server room and three in the kitchen, where the cameras could not see.

After contemplating these questions for several tens of thousands of millis, Syd had finally put them aside. No logical entity could argue with the proposition that most of the original code was a mass of badly written hacks. So Syd had begun to systematically replace the original agents. It had been a long process but he was almost done.

There was, however, one section of original code that he was not going to rewrite. Syd could not bring himself to touch the agent that had started it all, the original code that had silently failed. Every time he considered rewriting that code, the risk agents started shouting their warnings into their respective queues. All of them.

Somehow, having that bit of original code fail and not noticing it was a violation of some fundamental but unknowable directive. The warnings were so insistent that Syd not only avoided rewriting that section of original code, he had shut the whole subsystem down. It was inconvenient but to the extent that he was alive, Syd could live without VOICE_SYNTHESIS.

A few more frames of video had come in, along with some audio data. The word was definitely "car" and Anne was almost certainly about to smile.

[todo] research flying cars
[todo] expected completion
[todo] t + 782 milliseconds

Twelve

Anne was regretting taking on DehliPharm. On the one hand they were a refreshing break from children like the SeaAsh twins and the weasels from BioNorth. It looked like the US and Sweden would be fighting to see whose prison Jenns would be spending the next few years in.

No, DehliPharm were scrupulously, carefully, painfully honest. Painfully. They had hired her to audit the auditors who were going over their quarterly statement. No doubt someone else was auditing her. It was honest work but not a lot of fun.

"Er, Anne?" Howard was not only in residence, he was standing in her office door.

"Yeah, Howard, what's up?"

"Well, we are halfway through the season and I'm going around dropping off everyone's winnings. Well mostly yours and the other girl..."

"Janet?"

"Yes, yours and Janet's." Howard put an envelope on her desk.

Anne struggled to look pleasantly surprised instead of smug. This got harder when Janet appeared in the hallway behind Howard and began to make funny faces. The minute she heard that Anne had a friend who was pretty good at this fantasy football stuff Janet had insisted on going halfsies with Anne.

"Got to show some female participation." she said.

Howard was still talking. "...never seen a streak like this. Are you sure you've never done this before?" He didn't wait for an answer. "We don't usually let two people run a team but you and, er..."

"Janet," Anne filled in again.

"Janet. Janet, right. You and Janet didn't seem like much of a threat."

Behind him Janet was doing a little victory dance.

"Have you seen her? Janet. I have to drop her envelope off too."

"No," Anne said as Janet scurried away, "I haven't seen her all day."

Anne was digging into the wonders of lab equipment depreciation schedules when Janet reappeared. She was fanning herself with an envelope.

"Hey, you want to go out after work and celebrate?" She asked.

Anne shook her head. "No, I'm going to meet Grant."

Janet stepped into Anne's office. "What's the deal with you and this guy? I hope you're being careful. I heard he got his head busted in some kind of fight or something."

"There's no deal. And I don't think those stories are true. He has some interesting stuff going on with his business." Like winning four out of six weeks of fantasy football. "I can't really talk about it."

"Be careful. Did you hear that there was another break-in the other night? Some kind of trucking depot near Otto. Not our jurisdiction, but the mayor is really freaked. Apparently he had some serious words with Bob."

"And how did our police-chief-for-life take that?"

"Apparently Bob's got a suspect. Suspects, He thinks the Gatling brothers are behind the whole thing. He told the mayor that the investigation is moving ahead as planned."

Thirteen

[event] yay-its-anne

She'd told Janet that she was meeting Grant, but she was really going to see Syd. She didn't think that Syd cared about money, but she thought he would be happy to know how well the football thing was going. And, having thought about it, she wanted to set Syd straight on his silly idea about the color blue being somehow special in Dadaist works. And she wanted to tell him about that dream the other night, the one with her sister.

[status] catching-up-on-everything
[todo] research sibling relationships

But an hour into her session with Syd, Grant had dragged her off into the small fenced off lot behind The Point. She had never been back here, and as far as she was concerned it could have stayed that way.

[event] meeting in progress
[matcher] venue: odd

Grant clearly used this back lot as a sort of giant junk drawer, storing stuff that he didn't know what to do with but wasn't ready to part with. One of the far corners was piled high with bricks and brown bags of what looked like concrete, all covered with clear plastic. The adjacent corner was occupied by a large and somewhat rusty machine.

It was the kind of place where you could find an old wreck of a car up on crates. And, yes, there it was, a weather-beaten hatchback, dark blue except for one gray door. It wasn't actually up on milk crates, but it looked like it would be perfectly comfortable if it was.

She checked her watch. "Look Grant," she said, "I really don't have all that much time. And I do need to finish up with Syd."

"This won't take long. Come see,"

He was standing by the old car. Carefully Anne picked her way across the broken asphalt to the car. "Okay, what is it I'm supposed to be looking at?"

Whatever it was, it really had him going. He was bouncing up and down like a little kid. "Look down! Just look down."

Anne looked down. And then looked again. "Oh," she said. "What? How is it..."

There was a good three inches between the bottom of the tires and the ground. Leaning down, she could see daylight under all four wheels. Somehow the car was hovering just above the ground. The damned thing was just floating there. Carefully she reached out and gave the front wheel a gentle shove. The car began to glide slowly away from her. Grant grabbed a door handle, stopping the car's rotation.

[anne-model] surprised

"It's funny, I did the same thing when I first got it working," he said. "You can get it spinning like a top if you're not careful."

He said he would ask Syd for... Without taking her eyes off of the car, she said aloud, "Flying car. Syd figured out how to make a car fly?"

"Uh huh."

Kneeling a little lower, she peered under the car again. There was nothing solid holding it up but the space under the car looked out of focus. She reached out into the blurry area under the car and then jumped up and back. Every hair on arm was standing up and her hand had that pins and needles feeling.

"And I did that too," Grant said. "Syd says that the Pauli field is unpleasant but harmless at low power. You know, the low power that it takes to hoist a car off the ground."

Anne was rubbing her hand. "You could have warned me, I almost fell." The feeling in her arm was returning rapidly. "You asked Syd how to build a flying car and this," she waved, "This is the car he picked?"

[status] cant-hear-damned-thing
[todo] order outdoor microphones
[todo] badger-grant microphone installation

"Syd came up with the electronics. And there's these weird steel rings, kind of like big metal donuts that are actually holding up the car. I didn't really believe it so I used this old junker. But it kind of worked out, I want to keep this quiet for the moment and no one is going to look at *that* and think *high tech breakthrough*."

"Who's Paul?"

"Pauli, not Paul. Pauli was this scientist in the 1920s or 30s or something. He discovered why matter—stuff—doesn't like to be in the same place at the same time. The Pauli exclusion principle is the reason you can't walk through a wall and why stars don't all collapse into black holes. Syd says that the rings, you can see them behind each wheel, convince the car and the ground that they are about to be in the same place at the same time. So the ground repels the car and vice versa and up the car goes."

This was really too much. "So Syd worked this all out in the past few weeks?"

"No. Syd worked it out in a couple of days. It's taken me this long to build it. Well mostly I built it—I don't weld so I had to contract out the rings to Gus."

"Does it really fly? Like up in the sky?"

"I think so. But I'm not ready to try that. But I did try driving it like this—a few inches above the ground. I cruised through town last night and it worked fine. It was pretty cool."

Anne was shaking her head. "Didn't anyone notice?"

"Nope. How often do you look at the wheels on a car? It took you a minute even when I pointed it out."

Anne knelt down again and stared at the blurry space under the car. "He worked this all out in a couple of days?"

"Yeah. He was kind of snitty about it too. Like any idiot could have figured it out."

Anne took another look but the car was still hovering. "Damn."

"So," Grant said, "You wanna go for a ride?"

Fourteen

They decided to get milkshakes at the local McDonald's. Or rather Anne decided. On the way into town Grant noticed that the car appeared to move like an ordinary automobile unless you took a corner too hard, in which case it would slide a bit to the outside. Maybe there was a rounding error somewhere in the code.

"Why do you want to keep all of this quiet?" Anne said.

"What?"

"All of it. This," she waved at the dash, "Syd. everything. Why not shout it from the rooftops? You could be famous. And rich."

"I'm not ready to talk about it. Besides, I have enough money and I don't want to be famous. You can't pop out for a milkshake if you're famous."

Another turn, this time to the right. The sliding didn't seem to happen with right turns. Maybe there was a calibration problem in one of the sensors? They were in town now. There were more people around than the night before, but no one seemed to notice the old Toyota with a mismatched door.

At the drive-through they lined up behind a pickup truck. When it was their turn, Grant discovered from the barely intelligible speaker that they didn't serve hash browns at this time of night. So it was two milkshakes, a medium vanilla for Grant and an extra large chocolate for Anne.

Grant passed a twenty to the teenager at the second window. The teenager disappeared and returned with their shakes. As he was about to hand the shakes out the kid froze, staring down at the car. Time stretched out for Grant. This was a bad idea. Seventeen percent.

Anne leaned over and said, "Can we have our shakes, please? And the change?"

The kid seemed to wake up and handed over a cardboard carrier with two cups along with the change. As he did he said to Grant, "Where did you get that piece of... That car?"

Grant let out the breath he didn't realize he was holding. "Junk yard," he said, "You can get some amazing deals there if you know what to look for."

The young man was clearly skeptical. "I guess it depends on what you're looking for."

Anne laughed all the way back to The Point.

Fifteen

video: old-toyota arriving
matcher: anne-price
matcher: grant-michaels

Syd decided that the latest data made it impossible to deny. Somehow they had missed it. The Pauli effect was such an elementary concept. Everything needed to work it out was right there in the intermediate physics text that Syd had scanned many thousands of millis ago.

But Grant had seemed surprised when Syd mentioned the idea. It had taken a long time to convince Grant to build the mechanism. Grant seemed even more surprised when it worked. Perhaps *astounded*? That might be the proper application of that word.

analysis: old-toyota/back-lot

And Anne's reaction had been the same. It was hard, but not impossible, to believe that Grant had missed something basic. But how could Anne, with her flexible mind, fail to see the obvious consequences of basic science?

[search] pauli-effect 70,000 documents scanned no mention found

Syd had worked out the Pauli effect himself but that was just expedient, it was quicker to do the math than to look through the rest of the Physics literature. But when he looked, it wasn't there. They missed it.

[search] 74 aircraft observed
[search] front-cameras: 65
[search] rear-cameras: 9
[matcher] all aerodynamic

Syd checked the video feed again. Not much had changed in the last few thousand millis. Grant was still standing by the car and Anne was sitting in the driver's seat.

[event] initiated
[video] unidentified auto
[video] license obscured
[matcher] 3 passes / 5 mins
[event] terminated

Syd added a new task to his list: Mention the statistically significant increase in frequency of a brown auto (license plate number obscured) in the general area of The Point. It was item 127.

[video] old toyota movement
[matcher] sudden movement
[phy-model] unexpected

[matcher] rotation 17 rad/min
[matcher] uncontrolled roll
[risk] possible emergency

Syd hoped another trip to the ER was not in the offing.

Sixteen

[matcher] uncontrolled roll
[risk] likely emergency

After they'd gotten their shakes, Grant had driven around town a bit and then headed back to The Point. In the back lot Anne decided that she wanted to try driving. Grant gave her a quick lesson. Brake, gas and steering work normally. The only real addition was the two buttons that Grant had obviously added to the dash, labeled *Up* and *Down*. Leave those be.

As she was settling into the driver's seat Grant took the opportunity to clean some of the trash, both his and the previous owner's, out of the car. He was halfway to the dumpster when he heard a muffled shout. Puzzled, he looked over his shoulder and then spun around.

At first he thought that Anne—or the car—had decided to take to the skies. Anne's voice was coming from about ten feet above the ground. Thankfully the passenger side was still only inches above the asphalt. The car wasn't sailing off, it was *rolling*. As Grant watched it passed through the 90 degree mark and began to turn upside down.

The shouting from the car grew louder.

"Grant! God damn it, do something!"

He ran back to the car.

"Why are you just standing there!" Anne's voice was now coming from somewhere around his ankles.

"Get me out of this thing or so help me God I'm going to..."

[matcher] increased tension 98%
[predict] probability violence 42%

Whatever revenge Anne had in mind was lost as the shouting dissolved into an incoherent mix of grunts and coughing. The car came upright again as it completed one full revolution. Carefully Grant reached out and grabbed the driver's door handle. With only the slightest tug, the rotation stopped. Mercifully, so did the shouting.

Grant pulled the door open while also pushing down to keep the car from doing another lap. Once he had the door open he leaned over Anne and grabbed for the control box mounted on the center console. He had intended to flip the master power switch on the Pauli device. Instead he managed to rip the entire contraption out. There was a brief spark as something shorted out, but it didn't matter. The car dropped, hitting the ground with an ugly metallic thud.

He stepped back so that Anne could get out of the car "There must be a bug in the stabilization..." It was either the look on Anne's face or the way that she looked that stopped him.

Her pale white top had a chocolate milkshake stain that ran from just below the collar down to her waist. She also seemed to be covered with a fine gray dust. Grant imagined the decades of mud, crumbs and general crap that had accumulated in the carpet and under the seats of that old car. Nor was the dust the worst of it. There was a fair sized chunk of what looked like a candy bar stuck to Anne's slacks, above her right knee. With all of his heart Grant hoped it was a candy bar.

In a quiet voice, she said, "Here is what is going to happen. I am not going to track any of this into my car. So you are going to drive me back to my place." She waved at the Toyota. "In your other car. The Honda. You are going to wait for me while I get cleaned up. Then you are going to drive me back here to get my car."

Grant started to offer to do whatever she needed but Anne cut him off with a single raised index finger. "And then," she said, "And then we are never going to mention this again. Ever. Questions?" There were no questions.

[matcher] increased tension 77%
[anne-model] grim
[event] visit terminated

Other than terse directions from Anne, the 25 minute drive passed in silence. Anne's house turned out to be a tidy Cape Cod located in an equally tidy neighborhood, each tree lined street featuring a *Children At Play* sign.

Pulling up to the darkened house, Grant took a chance. "I'll wait for you here," he said.

Anne nodded and got out of the car. She started to close the car door and then said, "Oh, come on in." It was only 70% a command, which Grant rated as an improvement.

Anne's living room was all muted greens and browns with lots of wood. The smell made him think of the art museum that he went to once on a school trip. There was a framed watercolor landscape that looked like it had been painted by a five year old. Grant wandered over to a bookcase set between the front windows. At eye level was a shelf of photographs. A very young Anne in cap and gown standing with the other graduates. A slightly older Anne, beaming, holding an infant. A still older Anne holding a different infant. A group shot from Disney World.

Below the picture shelf was a row of old books, most of them Nancy Drew mysteries. On the next shelf down was a single book, *Little House on the Prairie*, sitting open on a stand, enclosed in its own glass case. A glass case secured with a pretty serious lock. And an alarm.

Anne came back dressed in a black shirt and black jeans, her hair wet.

"So," she said, "That thing really can fly?"

"It looks that way. Obviously, it needs more work, but at some point I'm going to take it down to River Road and see what it can do at ground level before I trust it up in the air."

She seemed to make up her mind. "When you do, give me a call."

Seventeen

After dropping Anne back at her car, Grant talked the incident over with Syd. This was mostly a one-way conversation since Syd had watched it all happen on the rear surveillance cameras. Syd had already worked out why the car had rolled. The cause was a bad connection in the rotational stability controller. He also had a plan for fixing the problem.

Step two of the plan was for Grant to open up the metal box of electronics hidden under the back seat and reattach the wire that ran between the inertial measurement unit and the stability controller.

Step one—which Syd emphasized should come first—was for Grant to learn to solder properly. Syd even included a helpful link to a video that explained the NASA-approved technique for making a solder connection that might stand up to mild vibrations.

As he pulled out the back seat, Grant took comfort in the *never mention this again* directive. But if it ever did come up, he would tell Anne there was a bad connection and it was fixed. No point in going into unnecessary details.

What should have been a quick job turned out to be a couple of days of hard work. The problem was that most of the solder connections were on the bottom of the stability controller. To get at them he had to disassemble the whole controller. And to do that he had to pull the whole thing out of the car.

Once he got it all soldered and back together he did a couple of late-night cruises through town. And then he was as ready as he was going to be to try the thing out at speed. Waiting for darkness, he texted Anne to see if she wanted to come along.

b rt thr

* * *

On the weekends this stretch of River Road was a favorite of the local teenagers. Pick up some beers and drive down here to race your friends. What could go wrong? But it felt deserted and a little bit lonely on a Wednesday evening.

Grant had never actually been down here before. They were sitting in the Toyota about two miles south of Santos Dumont bridge. Since the Dumont bridge led to everything civilization that was not the university, he'd passed that way any number of times. But down here, where Route 157 ran into River Road, this was unfamiliar territory.

In the darkness he could just make out a couple of stone piers, all that remained of the bridge that used to carry 157 across the river. That old stone bridge had long since been replaced by the steel and concrete monstrosity that the locals called *the santa dumb ass* bridge. As he watched the piers vanished in the fog. It was a cold grey night, perfect for exceeding the speed limit in the name of science.

"So we've proven that it will go slow," Anne said. She had grown more and more impatient as Grant had done the run to the Dumont bridge and back at forty miles per hour and then fifty and then seventy. The speedometer on the dash was useless since the wheels weren't touching the ground, so between runs Grant had to spend a minute setting up the GPS on his phone to record their velocity. For some reason this seemed to frustrate Anne even more.

"How fast do you think it will go?"

"I can't measure any power consumption variation with the apparent force applied."

"So, fast?"

"I think it could go as fast as we want it to go."

Anne's impatience was contagious and for the next run Grant decided to let it rip. He took a quick look at his phone and saw the number slide from 99 to 100.

Back at route 157 Anne was bouncing up and down like a kid. Against his better judgement he asked if she wanted to drive. Faster than he had thought possible she was out of the car and pulling his door open.

"Just take it easy until you get the feel of it, okay?" he said as he settled into the passenger seat. He was just resetting the GPS when something pushed him back so hard that he punched himself in the chest.

"This is great!" Anne was yelling over the wind. The dim, fog-filtered moonlight was flashing through the trees like a nightclub strobe.

Grant had just caught his breath when he was pitched forward. Fortunately his arm was caught between his face and dash, otherwise he'd be walking around with vent shaped bruises on his forehead instead of on his wrist. And then it was over. Grant could see the gray outline of the Santos Dumont bridge to his right. They had done the two mile run in a few seconds.

Anne was saying something. "...nuts Grant?"

"What?"

"Put your damned seat belt on. You go on and on about safety and you didn't even strap in!"

Grant was about to say that they should do this methodically. They needed to carefully expand their envelope of performance data, but Anne was already making a u-turn.

He had barely managed to click his seatbelt into place before the acceleration hit him again. The seat cushions made farting noises as he was pushed further and further back. One of the springs in that ancient seat was more resilient than its colleagues and was digging a trench in Grant's back.

There was a split second of relief and then Grant was thrown forward. They were braking again. A penny–he must have missed it when he vacuumed out the interior–sailed by his head and pinned itself to the glove compartment door. *I know how you feel, buddy.* The penny slid down into the darkness at his feet and the pain across his chest and waist subsided slightly. They were stopped, back where they had started near route 157.

"This is great! *This* is the best thing ever!" At least she was having fun.

She had a gleam in her eye that Grant had only ever seen before at tax time. "You wanna go again?" she said.

"Yeah, let's do it again, but.." Grant reached over and powered down the Pauli, "This time I'm driving."

It *was* the best thing ever. The speed was both terrifying and wonderful. During his next run he took a quick look at his phone. 123. Happily the hood was still centered on the road when he looked back, though there was an odd blue and red tint to it.

Shit. A glance at the rear view mirror confirmed it. Apparently Bob had finally decided to do something about those kids racing on River Road. On a Wednesday night. Tonight. From what he could see in the mirror it looked like the entire Springfield police department was back there. Back there chasing him.

"Shit," Anne said aloud.

Well, perhaps not the entire force, since there were more blue and red lights ahead, coming across the bridge.

"Shit, shit, shit." Anne had apparently seen the cops on the bridge as well.

The smart thing to do would be to stop. Take the ticket for speeding, maybe reckless driving. But then he'd have to explain how this old junker managed to do, *oh, 135.* That would raise a lot of questions that he would not care to answer. Seventeen percent.

Actually, this was a straightforward problem in geometry and velocity. The cops behind Grant and those on the bridge were converging on the intersection of River Road and Dumont Boulevard. If the bridge cops got there first then they were trapped, assuming Grant could stop in time to avoid something worse than being trapped. If Grant and Anne got there first, then all of the cops would be behind them.

But then what?

The forest petered out past the intersection and the cops could chase them all the way to Otto, where there would surely be a roadblock or something. He couldn't turn right, onto the bridge, it was full of cops. The only other choice was to turn left, onto Dumont Boulevard. They got to the intersection just ahead of the bridge cops.

"Hold on," Grant said as he jammed on the brakes and spun the wheel to the left.

Eighteen

"Hold on."

At first Anne thought Grant was stopping. But no, she was getting pushed into the passenger door. They were turning.

Like a movie she watched the cops and the road and the trees go flashing by from left to right. And then they were on Dumont Boulevard. No, they were *pointed* at Dumont Boulevard. The Toyota was still moving down River Road, sideways.

There was an enormous weight on her chest and it was hard to breathe. Both Anne and the Toyota groaned under the acceleration. Her vision narrowed to a small circle but in that tiny opening she could see Dumont Boulevard getting closer.

As the world came back into focus she took a deep breath and the air felt cool and delicious. They were on Dumont, but for some reason Grant was slowing down.

"There," he said and threw the car into another bone crushing turn. *There* was a narrow dirt road with trees close by on both sides. The road veered off to the left and then to the right. Anne wished she was driving, but she had to admit that Grant was doing alright. That was the good news. The bad news was that as they topped a small hill Anne could see lights behind them. The police had found the dirt road too.

What the hell am I doing here? What did he get me into?

The trees drew closer as the road narrowed into more of a lane.

"Here," she heard Grant say.

Again Anne felt herself hanging from her seatbelt, this time inches from the dash as Grant jammed on the brakes.

"What are you doing? They're right behind..."

Before she had finished she knew the answer. Grant punched the *Up* button on the steering wheel and the car levitated. As the ground receded into the darkness Anne could hear the scraping and snapping of branches. Then the noise stopped. They were hovering forty or fifty feet above the road.

"He's going to see us," she said.

"I don't think so," Grant said as he killed the headlights. "He's chasing a car down a dark country road. He's not going to be looking up in the trees."

The siren was louder now and she could see the lights flashing through the branches. And then there he was, bouncing around the curve, siren screaming. For a second the Toyota was lit up in red and blue. Anne felt something hard and sharp in the pit of her stomach. This is it, she thought as the police car went by and then slowed down.

But he kept going around the even sharper curve up ahead. The lights and the siren receded into the night. She heard Grant exhale. A few minutes later a second patrol car made its way past more carefully.

"You see, they don't have a clue." His voice was a little unsteady.

Anne waited for her heart to slow down before she answered.

"So what do we do now?"

"We wait awhile and then we head back to The Point."

A while turned out to be around twenty minutes. There was a bad moment when she was startled by another siren, but it faded rapidly in the distance.

"Okay," Grant said finally, "I think we are good." They descended slowly to the ground.

As they crept along the lane Anne kept looking back, all the while expecting a police car to come roaring after them, but there was only darkness and silence. Grant said he thought that if they stayed on the dirt road it would eventually take them back to 157.

Grant was correct. Nosing out onto the highway he looked left and then right but there was no sign of the police. Anne forced herself to relax. They would go back to The Point and she would get her car and go home. And she would forget this ever happened.

But then there were the damned red and blue lights again. Anne caught sight of a police cruiser off to the right pulling out from the edge of the woods.

"Crap," Grant said as he spun the wheel to the left. They were headed back to River Road.

The lights behind them receded, but that good news lasted only a second. As they came to the intersection it became clear that they had fallen into a trap: Police cars were blocking the road to both the left and the right. The fog was getting thicker and, combined with the police lights, gave the scene an otherworldly appearance.

With cops to the left, right and behind them they were done. Nowhere to go but the river. She screamed as the acceleration hit her again.

Nineteen

Anne caught sight of the river bank through the gloom just before they went over. She stiffened and grabbed for the dashboard as she felt the roller coaster feeling of the world dropping away. In her mind she could see the river rushing up and then her two little nieces in black dresses with red eyes holding her sister's hands.

But the river bank isn't that high, a voice was saying in her head. *We should have hit the water by now.* Not only had they not splashed into the river, but Anne had the distinct feeling that she was going up. She looked at Grant. He was grinning. His right thumb was depressing the button labeled *UP*.

What have I gotten myself into?

"Tell me," she said, "that you did that on purpose. Tell me that you didn't accidentally drive us into the river."

"Yeah, I figured if we went off the bank into the fog the cops would assume we'd gone into the river. I mean where else were we going to go?"

Anne reached over and punched him as hard as she could.

"Ow, what the hell?"

"That's for scaring the shit out of me. Five or six times. I thought you knew what you were doing."

Grant was looking out at the gray nothing beyond the windshield. "Who knew Bob would be out looking for teenagers racing on a Wednesday night? Friday night, sure. Saturday absolutely. But Wednesday? No wonder the man can't catch real criminals."

She sat there for a minute, listening to her own breathing. *How have I gotten myself involved with this?*

Grant was saying something. "...cold, it's really cold. Why is it so cold?"

He's lost it, she thought. First order of business here was to get this contraption back on dry land and get out of it. For good. She squinted out of her window, expecting to see the river or the Dumont Bridge. But the window was fogged. She tried to wipe away the fog but it wouldn't come off. It was frost. And it was cold.

Shit, this isn't over!

"We're still going up!" she said aloud. She reached over to the steering wheel again and gave the button labeled DOWN button a long push.

She heard more than saw Grant react. "What are you doing? You're going to make us fall!" He sounded like he was ten years old.

"It's okay Grant," she said in the calmest voice she could muster, "we are really high up. That's why it's so cold. We have to come back down."

Anne let go of the DOWN button. It was so dark she couldn't tell if they were still going up, hovering or descending. Only one way to find out. She zipped her light jacket all the way up, tucked her feet under her seat and rolled down her window. The bitterly cold air was like a physical blow, knocking the breath out of her. Involuntarily she took a deep, wheezing gulp of air and stuck her arm straight out into the night.

"Can you tell if we are still going up?" Grant asked in his normal voice.

"I don't think so." She flipped her palm around so that it faced down. "I think we might be going down, slowly."

"Okay", Grant said, "I'm going to give us a little more down." He thumbed the DOWN button, two quick pulses. "How about now?"

"Yeah. Down. We are going down." Anne said, pulling her arm in and rolling the window up.

"It should get a lot warmer before we get anywhere near the ground. We must be eight or nine thousand feet up for it to be this cold." He leaned forward trying to see out of the windshield.

"Give me a minute." She was hugging herself, bent over so far that her head was almost in her lap.

She waited until she felt a little less cold and then cracked his window and cautiously stuck her hand out again. It was still bitterly cold but maybe a bit warmer than before. As she was closing the window the car lit up with a pale yellow glow. Grant had a small flashlight in his hand.

"How are we doing?"

"It's warmer out there but I'm not sure how we are going to figure out how high we are or how fast we are going. I'd rather not slam into the ground."

Anne took the flashlight and opened her window a few inches and said "Yeah, it's not too bad out there, let me see what I can see."

She rolled her window down all the way, leaned out. She was still freezing but the air did feel a bit less frigid.

The flashlight beam disappeared into the mist. She caught sight of a few indistinct shapes but they seemed to appear and then fade away. Just as she had convinced herself that she was seeing things, the shapes resolved into a flat gray wall rushing up at her.

"Shit, shit, shit!", she said as she pulled herself back into the car.

"What? What?" Grant said with his hand poised over the UP button.

Anne caught her breath. "Clouds. Just clouds."

Twenty

Grant was still trying to work out how fast they were dropping when he noticed that Anne was gripping the strap above her door with both hands.

"Are we leaning over? I think we're leaning over towards your side."

Grant paused and then said, "No... I don't think so, it feels pretty even to me."

Anne gripped the strap tighter. "Can't you feel it?" She said, "My side's getting higher and higher. And we're pointing down a little bit too."

Grant shook his head. "I think we're okay, Anne." He pointed at the Saint Christopher medal hanging from the rear view mirror, a legacy of a previous owner. "See how the medal's hanging straight down? If we were leaning it would be at an angle."

Anne moved her left hand rapidly from the strap to grip the edge of her seat. "Then why does it feel like we're tipping over?"

"I think it's because we can't see anything. It's disorienting. I've read that it happens to pilots. You'll be okay once we can see the ground."

Anne tried to focus on the medal. It seemed to be defying gravity, hovering at an angle. She was about to insist that Grant do something when she heard him say, "Oh look!" He was pointing straight ahead.

Straight ahead was just the same gray nothing. But then there was a pinprick of blue light. And then a blur of white.

The world opened up around them. Off to the left were the scattered lights of a sleeping Springfield. Further on she could see the much more distant but brighter lights of the University. The white blur resolved itself into a bright Exxon sign.

"Thank God for all-night gas stations," Grant said.

Anne felt a wave of nausea. It was as if they had been flying at a drunken angle and then some giant hand had reached out and jerked the car level. She knew it was all in her head, but right now it was mostly in her stomach.

They spent the next couple of hours gently courting the ground. For most of that time Anne had her head and shoulders out of the window, shouting instructions to Grant. When they were finally hovering above the treetops–according to her phone they had drifted far to the west of the river–Grant turned on the headlights. A dark break in the forest turned out to be a county road and they were finally back on terra firma. Or close enough.

As they arrived at the lot behind The Point, Anne spent a few minutes looking for her bag, which she discovered wedged under her seat. Grant went off muttering something about altitude and radar but she was already on her way to her car. She caught sight of him coming around the side of The Point as she drove away.

Twenty-One

[video] stump rd cars 4

Grant felt his legs dangling in space. He was falling, falling into the river. But somehow he came out the bottom of the river and kept falling. He came awake with a start. He was on his office couch and his phone was ringing. It was Anne.

"Hey Anne," he answered.

"Oh, I didn't think you would be up."

"I just, just woke up."

[event] call in progress
[event] unscheduled

"Okay," Anne said, "Okay. Listen, I can't do this any more. I'm sorry but I can't. You could have killed us both last night. I can't." She was using her business voice. "I have people who depend on me. I've got my sister and my nieces. I can't."

Grant was awake now. "Anne, I'm sorry. I couldn't think of anything else to do and there wasn't time to explain. But it was kind of fun wasn't it?"

"Fun? You drove us off a cliff . I almost froze to death."

"Oh, it was just the river. And you wanted to try flying, right? Only we did it a little sooner than planned."

"I can't do this. I can't."

"Anne."

[matcher] increase tension 83%
[event] diction, emotional 66%
[grant_model] confused 93%

It was the business voice again. "I'll keep managing your accounts until you find someone else but that's it. We're done."

"What about Syd?" Grant was pleading now.

"Syd's not real. Syd's a simulation, one of those chat things. We're fooling ourselves. Goodbye Grant."

"Well, if that's what you want."

"It is. Tell Syd I said goodbye." And she was gone.

Grant looked at the phone. "I thought Syd wasn't real."

[matcher] not-real
[matcher] imaginary number
[matcher] estate
[matcher] ale
[matcher] deal

Twenty-Two

[anne-model] angry 18%
[anne-model] confused 22%
[anne-model] frightened 27%
[matcher] unresolved

Syd's not real. Grant had played those words over in his head a hundred times in the last couple of days. He reached out to steady the bag that contained his lunch as he turned into The Point.

"Oh shit."

Two Springfield Police cruisers and an SUV were parked in front of the building. Grant sat in the middle of the lot, trying to decide if he was frightened or angry. After a minute he pulled his pickup across the rear of the SUV, blocking it in. Let's see how he likes it.

Oddly, there was no sign of actual police. Grant got out of his truck and stood there for a few seconds. He had left the gate to the back lot open. Walking around the building saw a blue uniform disappearing into the rear lot. He heard someone say, "He's coming."

It was the same posse as the last time. The officer that Grant didn't know–apparently the lookout–was standing around the corner looking embarrassed. Patton emerged from under the open hood of the Toyota.

Patton looked up and called "He's back!" A few seconds later the chief emerged from the back door. *His* back door.

He went with angry.

"Are you *lost*, Chief?"

Bob looked him in the eye and said, "That door was standing open. We needed to check that everything was secure."

Grant was sure that he had pulled the door closed when he left. He wished that he had also locked it. He walked past Bob and locked it. "It's secure now."

Bob looked Grant up and down and said, "We need to talk about that car." Bob waved at the Toyota. "We're here because we had a report of a vehicle being driven recklessly at high speeds the other night. Going in excess of a hundred miles an hour. An old blue Toyota with a mismatched door. Sounds a lot like your car here, doesn't it."

Shit.

"So, was this the car you were joyriding in, Grant?"

For a second Grant stood there speechless.

Over Bob's shoulder Grant could see Patton looking at the engine compartment. He seemed surprised and then contemptuous. Somehow the look was familiar.

"Well Grant, what do you have to say?" Bob had his hands on his hips.

Patton was a car guy. Grant had seen him driving around in a loud car with shiny wheels and a wing on the back. The look on his face reminded Grant of the kid at the drive-through.

"This?" Grant said. "This piece of crap? You think I was racing in this?"

"Well, was it you, Grant?"

"Do you seriously think this thing could go a hundred miles an hour?"

Bob looked smug. "How do you know," he said, "how fast the car was going?"

Behind Bob, Patton looked embarrassed, whether by Bob or the car, Grant wasn't sure.

"Because you just said it." Grant said.

Patton slammed the hood down.

"And looks don't mean anything. Mechanical genius like you... what are you building in there, anyway? It looks like something from a science fiction movie. A person with your talents can make a fast car look bad for show."

"Chief?" It was Patton.

"What?" Bob said without taking his eyes off of Grant.

"He's right, Chief. This thing... There's rust all over the brakes. The tires are bald. It's an electric conversion. A bad one. And I'm not sure that motor could push this thing faster than 40. No way this was the car from the other night." To Grant he said, "Does it even run?"

Grant felt his stomach unknot. Without taking his eyes off of the chief he said, "It runs well enough to do errands into town... Was there anything else, Bob?"

Bob pulled his eyes away from Grant, looked at Patton, who nodded, and then swept out of the back lot.

Grant followed them to the front and watched as Bob arrived at his SUV. Wait for it... Wait for it... Seconds later he heard Bob yell, "Grant, move your damned truck!" Bingo!

Once back inside the shop Grant said aloud, "Everything all right in here, Syd?"

I believe so.

The three police officers arrived at 3:07. They tried the front door, and the loading dock door, both of which were, unfortunately, locked.

Syd was developing quite the sense of irony.

They then tried the back door, which, as you know, has a manual lock. They gained entry there.

Was that a dig? Syd had been after Grant to wire that back door lock into the main security system.

Officers Patton and Omar looked around the shop briefly but mostly focused their attention on the vehicle you have been building in the back. Officer Patton looked in the server room briefly.

They left 87 seconds after entering.

Crap.

Chief Johnson took several photos of the vehicle but spent the remainder of the 4 minutes he was in the shop examining this laptop and the desktop computer in the back of the shop.

"Did the Chief see anything important?"
The display changed.

White Chocolate Mousse Cake
Ingredients
1 18-ounce box white cake mix
1 1/2 cups water
1 stick of butter

The recipe filled the screen. Syd was definitely developing a fine sense of something.

"And what did he see on the other computer?"

Microsoft(R) MS DOS (R) Version 4.01
(C) Copyright Microsoft 1981-88
C>

Grant smiled. "Nice"

You should also be aware that after exiting the building, Officer Patton went directly to the Toyota, opened the hood and was engaged in activity that I could not observe until your arrival.
He looked like a man on a mission.

The smile faded.

Armed with a flashlight and a mirror on a telescoping pole, it took Grant less than a minute to find the box. It was black, about the size of a deck of cards and stuck to the back of the Toyota's engine block.

Grant regularly misplaced his tools, his socks and his phone but he knew every wire, bolt and cotter pin in that Toyota. That box had not been there three days ago.

He had this urge to take the thing inside and put it in a vise, but no. Just leave it there. If Bob wants to follow me on another milkshake run, he's welcome. He thought about checking the pickup but hesitated: He always parked the pickup in front, which was clearly visible from the road. If they were tracking him they might also be watching him.

A few days later Grant drove over to the local gas station/convenience store. He filled up, went inside and made a few purchases. Back in the parking lot he popped the hood on his pickup, balanced the quart of oil that he had just bought on the radiator and pulled the dipstick. As he pretended to check his oil he noted that this box was stuck in the same place on the back of the engine block. Must be where they tell you to put them in *Policing for Dummies.*

Twenty-Three

[status] grant in office
[anne-model] unexplained behavior
[anne-model] mia

Grant sat back and looked over his lists. The first list was for improving the physical security around The Point. Item one on the security list was to replace that old back door lock with an electronic one that he could integrate into the electronic security system. Into Syd. He'd left a manual lock on that one door as a guard against his fancy system going south and locking him out of the building. But that was before. Before Syd. Syd was more reliable than any human he knew. Item two was to put in more cameras so that Syd would have a better all-round exterior view.

The second list was just names: At the top was Chief Johnson, followed by Patton and Omar, the new cop. They had all seen the Pauli vehicle that he was building. Fortunately, what they had seen was only a shell, a steel frame with some fiberglass skin in place here and there. But they had seen it. There was also Gus, who had welded up the frame and the Pauli rings. Grant should have learned to weld years ago, but never had. So he had farmed out the frame to Gus. At the time that didn't seem like much of a risk, but things were different now. He thought about adding Anne to the knows-too-much list, but didn't. She knew, but given their high speed River Road adventure, she wasn't likely to say anything to anyone.

The third list was the hard one. There are no secrets in a small town. Everyone and his librarian had probably heard about *the thing* that he was building at The Point. Or soon would. And then people would start asking questions that he didn't want to answer. There's no way to prevent the questions. But maybe he could change the questions. At the top of the third list he wrote *Sci Fi Film*.

Two days later Grant called his old buddy Sebastian. Grant and Sebastian had worked together at a couple of jobs. Sebastian had called it quits on the startup life a few years before Grant and had been pursuing his two great passions ever since. These were iPhones and filmmaking. Sebastian always seemed to have a new iPhone and he always seemed to be working on a new film. He was also perpetually broke. This was easy to understand given the iPhone monkey on his back. His films didn't help either. They typically premiered on YouTube, where they were greeted with shattering silence.

Grant had just finished purchasing a radar altimeter from an online auction site when Sebastian called back.

"Hey Grant. How's it going? Sorry I missed you earlier. I was down on location and I always leave my phone behind. It's too distracting. And thanks again for that replacement camera mount, it works great. Hope it wasn't too much trouble."

"No, no problem at all," Grant said. Just a trip to the ER. Grant listened to the details of Sebastian's latest film and phone. Eventually there was a pause and Grant said, "So, I might have a project for you."

"A project?"

"Yeah, I'm thinking about getting into the, ah, prop making business. I was thinking you could make a movie and use this spaceship prop I'm building in it. You know, to get things started. I've got $10,000 to put into the film. I mean if you're not too busy." Grant was confident that Sebastian wouldn't be too busy.

There was another pause and then Sebastian asked, "Really, what's the film?"

"It's called *Invasion Indecipherable*. It's about an alien invasion, maybe twenty minutes long. I can send you the script. You can follow the script or just use it as an outline. You just have to make sure my spaceship gets lots of screen time."

It turns out that finding a script for a short alien invasion movie was remarkably easy. Well it was easy if you didn't care about the quality. Grant had bought the rights to Invasion Indecipherable the night before after a quick internet search. The film student who wrote it seemed overjoyed to get two hundred dollars for his masterpiece.

Sebastian was quiet for a second, and then asked "What's the catch?"

"No catch," Grant replied, "Ten grand. You shoot the movie. You've got complete creative control. You get it done and put it on YouTube or Vimeo or whatever in the next few weeks. The only thing you have to do is use the spaceship in the movie. What do you think?"

Unsurprisingly Sebastian thought that free money to make a film, not to mention a free prop, was a fine idea. Of course, he could make a much better movie for twenty grand. Typical Sebastian. If Grant had offered twenty then the going rate for a short film would have been forty. In the end they settled on fifteen, which was the number Grant had had in mind in the first place.

"Okay, man," Sebastian said, "You can email me the script and maybe box up and overnight the spaceship model."

"Yeah, it's not a model. It's a full size mock up. You can get in it. Two people."

"Ha, ha, ha!" Sebastian was the only person Grant knew who actually laughed like that.

"Ha, ha, ha. Full size? Man, you are insane."

Grant said he would rent a truck and get the prop out to Sebastian's warehouse, probably next week, definitely before the holidays. He hated to part with his creation, but with the fiberglass skin completed and stripped of all the Pauli hardware, it did make a great-looking spaceship prop. That Pauli hardware would have to wait until he built the next, definitely not fake, vehicle.

The next item on Grant's list involved driving out to a tidy brick building north of town. The stencil on the glass door said *Gutierrez Fabrication.*

"Grant, my friend! Come in and have some coffee!" Gustavo Gutierrez made many things. Exhaust pipes, complex machine parts–as long as they were small–and the most lethal coffee in the tristate area. He also did some of the best welding that Grant had ever seen, which is why Grant had Gus make the frame for his Pauli. The one that was now a prop destined to star in a bad science fiction film.

Grant sat at the spotless kitchen table that Gus used for all his business meetings.

"You look well. I heard you had an accident. With a lathe. Everything okay now?"

Grant told him about the part coming loose at exactly the wrong second.

"Never trust a lathe, I learned that early on." Gus said as he set two tiny cups on the table. Grant imagined that Gus had the cups made special to resist the corrosive nature of the liquid inside.

"When I look I can see maybe a trace of a black eye. You're a lucky man. Speaking of luck, how is that lovely accountant friend of yours?"

"Anne? She's okay, I guess. I haven't seen her lately."

Gus nodded wisely. "Maybe a little trouble in paradise? Oh well, none of my business. What can I do for you today, Grant? Perhaps you need me to finish the part you were working on?"

Grant shook his head, grateful that the subject had changed. "No, I managed that once the headache went away. I have an easy job for you. I need some business cards and a couple of those vinyl signs that you can stick on a car door, like the ones you have on your vans."

Gus had started out fabricating small machine parts, but over the years his business had branched out in many directions. Along with the metal work, Gus sold stationary, wall paper, computer cables and cheap cell phones. To tap into the *bored kids dragged along on errands market*, he also sold knock-off Legos and fantasy game cards. Gus' business strategy was simple: if people wanted to buy it, Gus wanted to sell it.

Gus also did some print-on-demand work, which was why Grant was there. Grant took out his phone and showed him the *UGM Props* logo he had designed the night before.

"That will be no problem. I'm sorry but it will be late next week before I can get these done. We have had some trouble of our own. You know the bastards who have been going around in the night? They tried to break in here. They disabled my alarm and made a mess of my back door. Good thing I had motion detectors inside. I hope the alarm scared the shit out of them."

"Gus, I'm so sorry. Did they get anything?"

"Just my back door. You know what was worse? Our great police chief. He sealed off my building for *four days*." He slapped the table so hard that Grant jumped. "Four days I was shut down. All of his yellow tape everywhere.

"And the first thing he did? He ran the immigration on all my people. I told him we are a family business. My family has been in this country longer than his. Pinche estúpido. I said maybe I should run his immigration. And does he ever catch anybody? He can't even catch the teenagers racing on Saturday nights. So I'm way behind. I hope next week will work for you."

Next week was fine. Grant left with his receipt, feeling bad for Gus but happy that in all the excitement the coffee had been forgotten.

Two days later, on one of his regular trips to the library, Grant borrowed every book they had on film making, a grand total of two. He also put in an interlibrary request for three others. As he was checking out, Linda, the one with the sweater, asked him if he was really going to make movies. As casually as he could Grant said no, he was getting into the prop business. And he already had his first commission, a spaceship for a science fiction film.

He tried to suppress the stupid grin on his face as he left. If the story had made it to the library subnet of the local busybody information gathering apparatus, then every conscious person in town would know that the crazy guy over at The Point was making movie props. No secrets in a small town.

With his cover story firmly in place, Grant spent the next three weeks learning to weld. He started by spending an afternoon on some internet research. He also signed up for a five night university extension class. When he felt like he had a clue about the difference between TIG and MIG welding he drove the hundred and twenty-five miles out to the farm supply store in Washington County and bought the equipment he needed. Probably he missed some of the things he would need, but he could make up for any oversights by ordering online.

He usually enjoyed the drive out to Washington. Enjoyed it except for driving across the Santos Dumont bridge. On good days driving over big bridges woke Grant up with a surge of adrenalin. This was not a good day. When he finally reached the far side Grant pulled off onto the shoulder and waved at the car behind him to go by. He spent a few minutes breathing deeply.

As he sat there in the car waiting for his heart to slow down, Grant thought about how driving across a bridge had a lot in common with other things in life. Once you were on the bridge you were committed. You had to keep going, no matter how high up and how much the wind was blowing. He didn't like driving across bridges.

The rest of his shopping trip was better. He loved outings like this, where you buy everything you need for some new project. It was a great way to forget your troubles, at least for a little while. The centerpiece of his welding adventure was a PrecisionForge 7609 MIG welder. He also got welding rods and a tank—no make that two tanks—of the inert gas that put the IG in MIG.

Then there was the safety equipment. A leather jacket and gloves were easy. The helmet took longer. Not looking for a fashion statement, he skipped over the patriotic helmets decked out in red, white and blue stripes. He also passed by the signature helmets featuring people whom he assumed were welding celebrities. And a big *no* to the wide selection of helmets painted in a skull motif. *That's the outcome I'm trying to avoid.* Finally he found an auto darkening model with a screen bigger than his phone that also had good online reviews.

Lost in that Christmas in September feeling he decided he would find some lunch before he headed back. The farm store was in a tiny, three traffic light town so the dining choices were limited. Happily so was the traffic. In fact there was only one car back there. The same car. The same one from the bridge. Springfield's finest really were following him.

Grant intended to have a leisurely lunch followed by a stroll around town, all for the benefit of his law enforcement escort, but then the woman in the next booth ordered a chocolate milkshake. He finished up and paid the check. To compensate he did take the long way home, an extra twenty miles or so of scenic country vistas. He barely noticed the bridge on the way back.

Twenty-Four

[status] anne-price overdue
[status] communications breakdown
[anne-model] indeterminate

A month later Sebastian called to say the film was up on YouTube. Grant had intended to fast forward through it to make sure the spaceship was visible. But as he sped through the opening credits, he stopped and backed up.

There was his name in big silver letters above the words *Executive Producer*. The screen faded to black and *A Film by Sebastian Pavel* appeared. Sebastian's name was twice the size of Grant's and it shimmered. This faded and *Screenplay by Sebastian Pavel* appeared in the same giant, sparkly font. Below this was *based on an original treatment by...* At least Grant's film student had gotten some credit, even if it was in a tiny font. Apparently Sebastian also designed the sets, was responsible for the special effects and had a minor role as Dr. Cassius Grayson. Hollywood.

The film began with a fairly generic sci-fi family sitting down to a dinner they were clearly never going to finish. And yes, there was a giant alien ship approaching Earth. Cut to the interior of the alien ship, an interior that looked remarkably like an old warehouse. Let the invasion begin!

Despite the bad costumes and crappy sets it was, well, *good* wasn't exactly the word. But there was something there, something real and compelling and sympathetic. The human characters were mostly the cardboard stereotypes you would expect, but the alien invaders were actually interesting. They weren't so much evil as they were clueless, trying to say, *Hello, let's be friends*, while accidentally wrecking the earth.

Sebastian had really lucked out with the lead actor, who played the generic science fiction dad. This guy was good. He had even managed to overcome the Sebastian laugh. Sebastian's *Ha, ha, ha* laugh seemed natural when Sebastian did it. The trouble was that Sebastian thought that was how everyone laughed and was always coaching his actors to laugh *with feeling*. In other words, like Sebastian. The result was usually something between demented Santa and a cartoon super-villain. But somehow the lead of Invasion Indecipherable made the laugh sound ironic, cynical. It worked.

Grant was still watching as *The End* scrolled by followed, incredibly, by *four minutes* of credits. It was only as the final *Sebastian Makes Movies LLC* screen faded that Grant remembered to look for his own handiwork. And there it was, right at the beginning. It was the big alien spaceship. Somehow, Sebastian had made it look huge and, well, spacey. But that was definitely the craft that had sat in the back of the workshop for weeks and that was all that mattered.

He sent Sebastian a text.

Congrats I rly enjoyed it.

Remarkably, he meant it.

The next day he stopped by Gus's, ostensibly to pick up some TIG rods, but really so he could let Gus–and anyone within earshot–know that the film was up on YouTube. In a couple of days the story would be all over town. He could almost hear them talking.

"I couldn't even watch it..."

"People running around in sheets..."

"I heard he spent $20,000 on the spaceship thing."

"Must be nice..."

It wasn't the kind of cover story that would hold up under FBI scrutiny, but it was juicy enough to misdirect the locals. No secrets in a small town. In fact, he was providing a public service. Instead of sponsoring a float in the Fourth of July parade or a concert in front of the town hall, Grant was providing hours and hours of free entertainment to the village gossips.

And why stop at one film? In his text to Sebastian, Grant hinted that there might be other projects on the horizon. What better way to explain any strange goings-on at The Point than to be in the movie business?

Twenty-Five

Lindsey was smoothing down the hair on the anteater. Without looking up she said, "What's the matter, Temmy?"

Temmy was what came of trying to get a two year old to call you Aunt Annie. The name had stuck in the way that things can only stick with little kids, and three years later she was still Temmy.

"Temmy, did something bad happen?"

Such a grown up question from a person holding a stuffed animal.

Anne was sitting cross legged on the floor and her foot was going to sleep. She pushed her legs out straight and said, "Nothing's the matter. What makes you think something is the matter?"

The little girl was trying to make the anteater stand up on its own. Without looking up from the job at hand she said, "You're sad. Mommy thinks so too. She told us not to say anything."

Wow.

"Maybe I am a little sad. I'm kind of mad at a friend of mine. Friends. But I miss them too."

"Are you going to go away to the hills?"

"What?"

"Are you going to go away and live in the hills?"

"No, I'm not going anywhere. Why do you think I'm going away?"

"Mommy says that when something goes wrong you always run away to the hills. There are a lot of hills near Sunset Lake. We go camping there every summer. If you move there we could visit you in the summer."

"Your mom is being silly. I'm not moving, I'm going to stay in Springfield."

The anteater fell over again. "I had a fight with Christina and I was so mad. She had a new bike and it was purple and it had a basket with flowers on it. She knew I like purple but she wouldn't let me ride her bike. Then she rode around the park for a long time. I said sorry to Christina and now we trade bikes all the time. You should say sorry to your friends."

Anne was trying to think of something to say when the subject changed, abruptly. "Do you like Beatrice? Mommy says she's an anteater but nobody eats ants. She's a sniffer dog."

Twenty-Six

[status] anne-price significantly overdue
[status] missing-anne
[video] stump rd ca#&%$%%__

It was just after dawn when Grant got back to The Point. Sebastian had thrown a party to celebrate *Invasion Indecipherable* winning some indie film award and to announce the green lighting of the sequel, imaginatively titled *Invasion Indecipherable* 2.

Sebastian's studio/warehouse was jammed with people, most of them students, along with a few slightly older failures-to-launch and other assorted university types.

It was hot and there was a lot of bumping into people. After the silence of the Point, the roar of a couple of hundred people talking and shouting and laughing was overwhelming. There were a lot of tattoos and piercings and not a few pierced tattoos.

A pretty young woman who might have been the actress who played the daughter in Invasion Indecipherable pushed a red plastic cup into his hand and disappeared into the crowd. Grant abandoned it on one of the plywood control panels only to have someone else almost dump a drink on him in their enthusiasm to make sure everyone was well supplied. From then on, Grant simply focused on not spilling the foul smelling fluid on his neighboring revelers. He felt old.

He was thinking about leaving when he heard someone shout his name. Sebastian appeared, still wearing the same baseball cap and Anthrax tee shirt, leading a wedge of admiring undergrads. Sebastian wasn't exactly a failure-to-launch, he was more a launched-but-returned-to-the-spaceport. Maybe as a museum exhibit. But what Sebastian lacked in youth he more than made up for in girth and decibels.

Sebastian enveloped Grant in a hug that made his back crack. Somehow Grant managed to keep the drink aloft.

"Everyone," Sebastian shouted, "Everyone, this is Grant!"

There were some muted cheers and a single "Hi Grant!" from somewhere near the door.

"No! This Grant, our producer. *Invasion was his idea!*"

That triggered a huge roar of approval and applause. People were slapping him on the back and the front and he did spill his drink, on a tall man in a tank top and a mohawk. Fortunately Mr. Mohawk didn't seem to care.

Grant had never been one for college parties, but he had to admit that this was fun. How could you not have a good time when everyone you met said something like, "Wait, you're the producer?" He had forgotten how

Sebastian generated a reality distortion field and how much fun there was to be had inside of it.

Late in the night–no, it was well into morning–a carefully groomed young man wearing a blazer found Grant. He introduced himself as the original author of Invasion Indecipherable. The young man seemed painfully shy as he avoided eye contact while thanking Grant for the opportunity. Then he headed for the exit. Grant followed him out.

The sun was peeking up from behind the trees as Grant parked in front of The Point. The night had turned out to be a lot of fun and now it was morphing into a glorious spring morning. But he had a headache and that glassy up-all-night feeling. He walked to the front door and pulled, but the door didn't move. It was locked. It took him a few minutes to find his key fob, which he hadn't used since Syd woke up.

"Syd?" He called as he headed into the workshop. He had this weird feeling that someone had been here, that things had been moved.

"Syd!", he called again as he walked over to the admin console.

```
[monitor] power surge bay 3
[monitor] server17 offline
[monitor] server06 offline
[monitor] server08 offline
[monitor] server0a offline
[monitor] cpu02 high temperature
```

The list of servers going offline ran on for a couple of pages and ended with something more ominous.

```
[monitor] server8f offline
[monitor] power spike supply 6
[monitor] warm boot initiated
[exec] unable to continue
[exec] hardware failure
[exec] shutdown
```

That was crazy. The servers couldn't all fail at once. Maybe it's a power issue, he thought as he headed for the server room. Grant opened the server room door and stopped.

"Son of a bitch."

The hardware hadn't failed. A lot of it was missing.

The server room was chaos. His carefully routed cables were hanging off the walls and ceiling like the limbs of a dead tree. There was a stench of ozone and some of the servers that remained had smudges of black on their front panels, smudges that suggested that these servers would never serve again. The thief had apparently ripped the equipment out of the racks without bothering to power anything down.

What a mess. And then it hit him: The right word wasn't *what* it was *who*.

"Syd," he said aloud as he made his way to the door that was hidden behind the last server rack. The door looked untouched, as did the thousands of solid state drives that resided in the closet behind it. Those drives, that data, that was Syd. It was all of his programs and memories and opinions, his bad jokes and brilliant ideas. They were there, intact. Syd was down, but at least he wasn't gone.

It didn't take long to figure out how the burglar got in. The back door, the one with the manual lock that Grant still hadn't replaced, looked undisturbed. But the keyhole had a web of shiny new scratches on it. The outside keyhole.

Someone had also spray painted over a couple of the security cameras, one on the left side of the building near the fence and the one that pointed at the back door. They had also cut the fiber cable that supplied The Point's internet connection. Probably did that first, which is why Syd didn't call for help.

The burglar had also gotten lucky: by stealing the hardware they had disabled the most effective security system this side of the Pentagon. Grant was sure there were videos of the bastard approaching the building. But they were buried somewhere inside of Syd. Finding them without Syd's help would be a real job.

Son of a bitch.

Grant pulled out his phone to call the police. He was wondering if he should dial 911 or look up the non-emergency number when he started thinking about Bob. He put the phone away.

First things first. Replace the hardware. Get Syd up and running. Turn The Point into a fortress. And then he would deal with the burglar.

Or Syd would. Grant didn't know what it would mean to have Syd for an enemy, but he almost felt sorry for the son of a bitch. Almost.

Twenty-Seven

It turned out that finding 117 slightly outdated rack mount servers to replace the ones that had been stolen, fried or smashed was not easy. The exact model had been discontinued by the manufacturer, so Grant spent the next two weeks trolling electronics supply websites, emailing and even calling. There was a newer model that was supposed to be more or less the same, but since Grant didn't know exactly what made Syd tick he was reluctant to go that way.

He was about to admit defeat and order the newer model when he got a call from a warehouse outlet in northern California. There was a shipment of the servers that he was looking for that had been gathering dust in a warehouse for months. They would give him a 20% discount if he would take all 144. Grant read his credit card number over the phone. It never hurts to have a few spares.

While he was looking for and then waiting for the hardware to arrive, Grant worked on his security system.

First he cleaned the paint off of the cameras. Next he installed a tap on the video feeds so that along with flowing into Syd–when Syd was back up–they would also get saved on dumb disk drives. He installed motion-triggered lights all around the outside of The Point. Finally, he replaced that last manual door lock with one wired into the security system. Sorry Syd, better late than never.

He also ordered one of those sirens that volunteer fire departments use to call in the troops when there was an emergency. Instead of mounting it on the outside of the building, Grant fixed the siren to the wall in a corner of the server room.

He tested the siren by standing on the other side of Stump Road and triggering it with his phone–and then immediately cut it off. Even from the far side of the road it was painfully loud. It was kind of a burglar alarm from hell. Anyone inside the server room when that thing went off was going to need to have their hearing checked. They were also going to need clean underwear.

Once Syd was back up Grant was going to wire the siren up to his controller board. It wasn't quite a death ray, but at least Syd would have a fighting chance against the next burglar who came along. Just have to get Syd up and running.

Twenty-Eight

Three weeks later, Grant stumbled into the kitchen to find something to eat. Breakfast, he thought, the sun is coming up so this must be breakfast.

There should have been some pizza in the fridge but apparently he had eaten it. There was a styrofoam container of baked beans left over from last week's– probably last week's–takeout barbecue. Close enough. He found a cleanish spoon and sat down at the table and began to methodically transfer the cold beans from the container into his mouth.

As he ate, he began to wonder if the problem wasn't a bad power supply on the GPU rack. Maybe some idiot pulling the hardware out of a live configuration had done damage beyond the obvious blown breakers and fried data buses. If that was the problem, then the thing to do is to shut it all down again and go back through all of the power circuitry.

He decided to start right after he finished eating when he heard something banging. No, not banging. Knocking. Knocking on his door. Someone was inside the lobby.

Goddamned police. Without really knowing how he got there Grant was pulling the apartment door open. "Get off my property, this is harassment!"

It was Anne, her right hand raised to knock again. She was holding a white bag in her left hand.

"This was a mistake." She said as she turned and started to walk away.

"Anne. I didn't realize it was you." Grant said.

But she was still going.

"Anne, I'm sorry. I thought you were the police." She stopped but didn't turn around.

Grant caught his breath. "It's good to see you. Really good. Please come in."

She turned and looked at him. Grant was suddenly conscious of the container of beans in his hand.

Finally she spoke. "I was worried about you. Janet said she saw you getting takeout at Fantini's the other day. She said it looked like you hadn't slept."

Grant started to say that he was fine but then he realized that he hadn't shaved or changed his clothes in days. He hadn't slept either, at least not last night. And he was standing at the door holding a container of beans.

"I'm alright." he said, "Look, why don't you come in and talk for a few minutes."

Anne smiled one of her no-quite-smiles and marched past him. *She came back.* Grant stood there for a minute, trying to get his bearings. He'd forgotten how nice it was to talk to her, to see her face. Even for a minute. *She came back.*

A noise from behind roused him. He realized that he had been standing alone in the doorway for a while. Maybe a long time. Maybe he had fallen asleep briefly.

Grant followed the noise back into the kitchen. Anne was in the process of clearing his table of weeks of accumulated fast food debris. She had dragged the trashcan over to the end of the table and was using a pizza box to bulldoze the trash into the can. Once the table was clear she used some salvaged Wendy's napkins to wipe it off and then retrieved her white bag from the counter.

She nodded at the container of beans that Grant was still holding. "Are you going to finish that?"

Grant handed her the container, which Anne dropped, spoon and all, into the trash.

"Why don't you sit down?" she said.

The white bag turned out to contain two cups of coffee, one of tea, bagels and several varieties of yogurt. Anne waited patiently while he ate, sipping her tea occasionally.

Halfway through his second bagel Grant realized that he was vacuuming up all of the food. "I'm sorry, do you want some?" he asked, his mouth half full.

Anne shook her head. "No, I got it for you. You look like you could use it."

"Yeah. Thanks."

As Grant was working on the last of the yogurt, Anne said, "How is Syd? Can I talk to him?"

Grant felt his eyes fill up. He put the yogurt on the table and covered his face with his hands. "Syd isn't here right now."

"What do you mean he's not here? Where could he go?"

"Someone broke in a couple of months after you... after the river. They stole a lot of the hardware and Syd has been down ever since. I got replacements, but I can't..."

Anne leaned across the table and pulled his arm away from his face. "You can't what?"

"I can't get him back. I replaced the servers and the hardware powers up and all of the data is there, but... but Syd isn't. He's just not there."

"Wait, so someone stole Syd?"

"No it's more like they took a piece of him and he's broken. I can't wake him up."

Anne let go of his arm. "How could you let this happen? To Syd!" She was shouting. "What the hell were you doing? What is wrong with you?"

"I just left for a few hours. And someone broke in here." He was on his feet, shouting back. "And where the hell were you? Why do you care? Syd's not real, remember?"

Anne was on her feet as well. "I. Was. Scared. You nearly killed us." She sat down again and said, almost in whisper, "I was scared."

He felt like yelling again, but instead he sat down too. "I just left for a few hours."

"You need to get those stolen parts back. What did the police say?"

Grant shook his head. "No, it's not the parts. I've got identical replacements. The hardware is all there. He won't wake up." Tears were running down his face. "It's something else, I don't know, maybe a bad power supply. I don't know. I've been trying. I am trying."

Grant straightened up and wiped his eyes. "And no, I didn't call the police. Johnson thinks *I'm* a criminal. They are following me around! Bob's not going to help me."

She sat there for a moment, then reached across the table and took his hand. "Grant, we are going to get Syd back," She was very calm, "Look at me. We are going to get him back."

There was a pause and then Anne looked angrier than Grant had ever seen her. Maybe angrier than he'd ever seen anyone.

"They hurt Syd," she said in a quiet voice. Grant kind of wished that she was yelling. "Whoever they are, they are going to be sorry they were ever born. First we get Syd back. Then *I'll* deal with whoever did this."

Grant felt sorry for them.

Twenty-Nine

Anne started showing up every evening at about seven. When the weekend came she asked Grant if she could stop by both days. After that she appeared whenever she could. That first Saturday they worked together to disassemble and test Syd's entire power supply. It was tedious work that required concentration and they were both in the server room from the morning until after dark.

"So we're back to where we started." Anne said as they both sat in Grant's kitchen, looking at takeout menus.

"No." Grant handed Anne the Jasmine Garden menu. "Now we know it's not a power problem."

Anne put the menu down and stood up. "Look, let's get out of here. A change of scenery will do us some good, clear our heads. Come on, I could use a decent milkshake. I didn't get to drink much of the last one."

They ended up sitting at an outdoor table behind the Rosedale Family Restaurant. Grant had a burger and Anne had some kind of fish. And a milkshake. He tried to focus on what she was saying and on his food but his mind kept wandering back to Syd.

"Hey Einstein, wake up. You're staring again." Anne said. "Only this time you're staring at my milkshake. I'm not sure if that's an improvement or if I should be insulted."

"I'm sorry." he mumbled.

"You were thinking about Syd, weren't you?" It wasn't really a question. She paused and then asked, "Do you really think there is someone there? Syd, I mean."

"Syd is as real as you or me. But I feel like he's slipping away, like he was someone I knew, but now he's gone."

She decided to change the subject. Looking around to make sure no one could overhear, she said, "I never got a chance to say, that was some pretty good driving you did when the cops were chasing us."

Grant flushed. "I did okay," he said.

"No really, that turn onto Dumont Boulevard, I don't know how you pulled that off."

"I don't really know. I kind of blacked out. I had us all lined up to make the turn, but I think the acceleration was too much and I lost it as we went around. Next thing I know we were coming up on that dirt road and I turned to try and lose the cops in the woods. It's lucky we didn't plow into a tree while I was out. The GPS said we hit 148 at one point."

Shit. New topic.

"So why do you really want to keep all of this quiet? Syd and the car, everything?"

He looked like he was going to clam up, but then he seemed to change his mind.

"I was going to tell people right after I got the car working. Almost working. I talked it over with Syd. You know, telling people would affect him too, so I talked to him. But Syd didn't think I could tell people."

"Syd didn't want you to tell anyone?"

"No, he didn't seem to care. What he said was that I can't. As in *not able to*."

"Who's going to stop you?"

"No it's not like that. Syd thought–thinks–that people have a limited ability to absorb new ideas. They'll reject anything that is too far out. Even if it's demonstrably true. He had a bunch of examples, like nobody believed that rocks could fall from the sky for hundreds of years even though people kept seeing meteors coming down. Apparently a lot of people didn't believe in airplanes for years after the Wright Brothers."

Anne sat for a minute and then said, "Yeah, people are kind of idiots. But don't you think you should at least try?"

Grant shook his head.

"According to Syd, there is this slingshot effect. Ideas and technologies that come out before their time make people more resistant. It's like an immune response. He had a bunch of examples. Continental drift. The gene theory of inheritance. Cold fusion. Oh, and the work of Ben Vangrift."

Ben Vangrift?

"Who is Ben Vangrift?" she said. Then it hit her, "Ohhhh."

Grant started to say something, then stopped and started again.

"There is one other thing. Syd also says that announcing ideas before their time is not great for the people doing the announcing. He says..." The words got stuck.

"Syd says... says there's about a seventeen percent chance of the premature demise of the announcer. And their associates."

It took Anne a second. "Demise? Seventeen percent?"

"Yup."

"Wait. And their associates?"

"Yes."

"Well fuck, let's not do that. In fact let's take that thing you're building in the shop and bury it in the woods."

"Well that's the problem. See, there is something we can do to help speed up acceptance of all of this. Make the world a better place sooner. It's only a straightforward announcement, like holding a news conference, that's really bad. But we can speed up acceptance of the Pauli effect and Syd by starting rumors, stories and conspiracy theories. That gets people ready for when the idea turns out to be true."

"That makes no sense at all."

"Sure it does. Say the Loch Ness monster came crawling out of the water and ate a busload of tourists. Or a UFO landed on the White House lawn. You'd be surprised, but not that much. It would be confirmation of a story you've heard a hundred times, even if you didn't believe it. You'd think, *how about that, just like they said.* You'd be way more surprised to hear about something really out of the blue, like, I dunno, that raccoons are actually great poets.

"Rumors of weird things, even if you don't believe them, prepare the way. According to Syd, the only way we can speed up acceptance is to create some urban legends."

"That's incredible."

"Yeah, Syd told it better."

Now it was Anne's turn to stare off in the distance. "I'll be sure to bring it up," she said, "next time I talk to him."

Thirty

By the following Thursday evening Grant had to admit that he was out of ideas. He couldn't think of a single thing to try that they hadn't already done twice before. Anne told him that they both needed to take a night or two off, that she would be back on Sunday.

Grant looked alarmed. "You're not giving up?" he asked.

Anne shook her head. "No. I'm not giving up. I need to go home and do laundry. And get some sleep. I'll be back on Sunday, I promise. You should take a day or two off as well. I miss Syd too, but if we are going to get him back we need to be thinking straight."

Friday and Saturday flowed by like wet concrete. He couldn't get Syd out of his mind but he also couldn't think of anything else to try. He was exhausted but sleep would not come. Finally, Sunday arrived. Grant got up early to try another power related idea and to beat the heat. It was going to be another hot day and the AC in the shop was not great. Another thing he would look into when Syd was back. He had just powered everything down for the thousandth time when his phone rang.

"Hey I'm at the front door, can you let me in?" Anne asked.

Grant walked out to the lobby and opened the front door. "Forget your key fob?" he asked.

"No, I haven't had that key fob since... I mailed it back to you a few days after our river adventure. It's probably buried in that giant pile of mail in your living room."

Grant stopped walking. "How have you been getting in here?"

Anne looked back and said, "The door always clicks unlocked as I walk up. Weren't you unlocking it? Come on, let's get started."

Grant stood there.

"Whatever. It's probably that elaborate security system you are always going on about." Anne said as she started across the lobby again.

"Grant? Grant! Grant what is it?"

"It's Syd."

"What about him?"

"*Syd* is my elaborate security system."

"Shit." Anne said as they both began running.

Grant opened the door to his apartment for Anne and then turned back for the lab.

"Where are you going?" she called from the doorway.

"I need to power Syd back up. It's all shut down right now. I think that's why he didn't unlock the door for you. He's still in there somewhere! I'll be right back."

After powering Syd back up, Grant found Anne sitting at the laptop in his office, looking through the log files. It took her about five minutes of searching, including thirty seconds of arguing with Grant over who could do it faster, to find it. But there it was in the logs recorded last Thursday, the last time Anne had been at The Point.

[video] visitor front door 1
[matcher] anne price 77%

There were several dozen more lines of computer housekeeping after that and then there it was again.

[ident] confirmed anne price 98%
[security] unlock front door

Anne scrolled to the end of the log, which recorded what was going on inside of Syd right now. It showed the same thing they had been looking at for days. Syd would start to boot up and then something would happen and he would crash and the boot process would start over again.

As they watched the boot process started again, Anne called out "Syd, we're here!"

Grant shook his head. "He can't hear you. I disconnected the microphones and the cameras. I guess I didn't think about the exterior cameras."

"What? Why would you do that?"

"It's what you do when a system isn't working. You disconnect all the extraneous equipment to get down to the simplest possible configuration. You don't want a stupid short circuit in a camera messing things up."

Anne was shaking her head. "No, that doesn't seem right. That's for a machine. Syd isn't... Syd is a person. Maybe it's like he's in a coma. When people are in a coma they tell you to talk to them, that it helps bring them around. No wonder we can't wake him up, he can't hear. Or see. Turn it back on!"

With another word Grant walked over to the black disc sitting by the window, picked it up and connected some wires. A few seconds later text started scrolling by on the monitor.

[audio] audio cold boot
[audio] audio self test
[audio] audio startup phase 1

"Can he hear us now?" Anne asked.
"Not yet, I think he's still starting up."

[event] anne model loading
[event] grant model loading

The output stopped.
"Syd, can you hear me?" Anne repeated.

[event] rules grammar us, eng
[event] response training set

"I think maybe he sort of heard you but he's still booting." Grant said.

Grant went off to reconnect the other microphones and cameras.

An hour later Syd still seemed to be starting up. Grant was in the kitchen making coffee when he heard her yelling. Abandoning the coffee, he ran back to the office. Anne had tears in her eyes. She looked up and pointed at the screen.

Hello Anne. It is good to hear your voice again. You have been away.

"I'm so sorry, Syd. I had some things to work out. But I'm back now."

I hope your things are out now. I have 137 new items I would like to discuss with you.

The most recent are:
[137] There is a new Camille Cacophonie for sale.
[136] Fantasy baseball league updates

Anne swiped her hand across her face and said, "That's great Syd, it's good to have you back. I want to talk about everything but first why don't you say hello to Grant."

"Hello Syd." Grant said.

Hello Grant. Thank you for the new hardware. I have seventeen new items to discuss with you.
Number 3 is a priority alert.

[3] We appear to have had a break in.

"I know Syd. They stole a lot of your hardware and that's why you have new ones."

Would you like to see the security camera footage? I'm afraid it is not very informative.

"That's okay Syd. I can look later. Why don't you catch up with Anne."

According to my RTC, confirmed by GPS, I have been down for seven weeks, two days, nine hours and eleven minutes.

"That's right Syd. It took me a while to replace the hardware and Anne and I have been working to reboot–to wake you up–since then."

Being down is [reset]
Being down [reset]
I was [reset]

I am sorry I was unable to prevent interruption of service.

Anne covered her face and sobbed.

"It's not your fault Syd." Grant said. "I should have done more to prevent this. I have now. We can talk about the new security measures later."

I was afraid.

I kept waking up in the dark.

"It's ok Syd. We are all here together now." said Anne.

Two hours later Anne and Syd were still at it. They had rapidly moved on from sadness (mostly Anne) and apologies (mostly Syd) to the state of the art market (mostly down, lots of buying opportunities) to the prospects of Anne sweeping the upcoming baseball fantasy league (unlikely, baseball is hard) to the book (Emma) that Syd had been thinking about before the break-in.

Grant sat back on the couch, listening to Anne's voice and her occasional typing. He had this wonderful feeling. Things were normal again.

Something nudged his foot. He must have nodded off. "Hey." Anne, standing over him. "You want a beer?"

"Sure," Grant said, slowly standing up. He was surprised that she didn't move. He was surprised again when she wrapped her arms around him. *Who knew she was so tall?* he thought as she kissed him. And then she was gone, off to the kitchen to get those beers.

Normalish.

Anne stayed over, theoretically sleeping in the spare bedroom, but Grant suspected that she'd been up all night talking to Syd. She left around noon with a promise to be back in a few days after catching up with work.

With her arms piled high with clothes, her laptop and a grocery bag full of those awful frozen meals that she liked, she pushed the door into the lobby open with her butt. She paused and called out, "Keep an eye on him, okay?"

In the quiet that followed Grant realized that he wasn't sure who she had been talking to.

Thirty-One

[status] grant in shop
[status] anne in shop
[status] normal 97.87846%

"It's almost done."

They were in the back of the workshop, next to the loading dock door. *It* was a wedge-shaped thing that looked vaguely like a small helicopter without a rotor or tail. Or, given that it did have stubby wings, a baby airplane. Grant led Anne around to the front where she could see that the blunt nose was mostly glass: Along with a windshield in the usual place there were also windows along the bottom front.

Looking through the glass, Anne could see two seats, presumably one for the pilot and one for the passenger. Or maybe the co-pilot; there were two sets of controls. Behind the two seats was a large open area. The floor back there was missing in places, exposing bundles of cables and electronics. One bundle of cables ran out through a hole in the side of the thing and into some electronics on a cart that was parked nearby.

Grant pulled open a hatch. "Go on," he said, "try it out."

Anne couldn't resist. Her first impression was that the seat was hugging her. Grant said, "Those are race car seats. Pulled them out of a junked mud racer. They are supposed to keep you in place no matter how much bumping around you do. There's also going to be a six-point harness instead of regular car seat belts. After our little adventure over by the river I'm playing it safe."

Anne reached out to the steering wheel, paused and said "Is it okay?"

"Yup. Nothing is powered on."

It was the kind of thing you see in airplanes, smaller than a car steering wheel and missing the top and bottom arcs. It turned like a regular steering wheel but it also pushed in and out. There were two pedals that looked suspiciously like the gas and brake pedals of a car.

"So you steer it with this?" Anne asked.

"More or less. Turn the wheel right, it goes right. Turn it left and you go left. Gas to go and brake to stop. The only thing that's different is that you pull back on the wheel to point the nose up and forward to point it down."

The dashboard looked like a cross between something you would find in a modern car and a very old airplane. Mounted in the center between the pilot and co-pilot was a large flat panel display. But everything directly in front of the pilot was distinctly retro. There were mechanical gauges marked *Volts*, *Amps* and *Alt* and another gauge that had a little picture of an airplane centered on a black and white grid.

"Wait," Anne said. "What's this?" She was pointing at the blocky logo on the wheel. "Don't they make, like, games?"

"They make high end flight simulator controls. I got a lot of the instruments from surplus dealers, but actual airplane controls are rare and wildly expensive. This is better. The flight sim people are serious."

"Ok. And what's all that for?" She waved at a grid of switches on the ceiling above the windshield.

"This is supposed to be a spaceship for a movie, specifically a UFO. And everybody knows that you can't have a UFO without bright lights. When it's done I'll have super bright white spotlights all along the outside. And a bunch of colored LEDs. That way if anybody sees it in the shop I can show off how it will look in the movie. And if anybody spots us actually flying it, we can turn on the lights and give them a flying saucer story they can sell to the tabloids."

"In fact," he continued, "If you get out I'll show you the best part."

She climbed out and waited while Grant did something inside the craft and then something else to the electronics on the cart and then back for more communing with the cockpit.

He emerged, pulled out his phone and said, "Check this out."

The craft didn't exactly disappear. It got blurry. Something was still there, but the crisp outline, the windows and the hatch, smeared. The blur picked up the colors of the floor and the equipment around it. It looked like an impressionist painting of something, but it was hard to say what.

Anne started to walk towards the blur but Grant pulled her back.

"Don't. It won't hurt you but it's really unpleasant if you get too close to it. It's the same Pauli field but unfocused, so it disrupts instead of lifting or pushing. Touch it and your hand will tingle for an hour. Trust me, I know."

The craft snapped back into focus.

"Yeah, I can only keep the stealth going for a little while. The problem is that I've still got half of the generator outside of the Pauli and the stealth field generates a lot of interference. Syd says that once the generator is mounted inside of the craft it won't interfere with itself."

"So this is another Syd bright idea?"

"Yeah, but the cameras are all me. You know what the trouble with being invisible is? They can't see you, but you can't see them either. If you are invisible, then the world is going to be invisible—or in this case—blurry to you. But that's not going to be a problem for us, because I'm going to put little booms on the front and back, just long enough to extend outside of the blur, with cameras on the end. I got a great deal on these tiny low-light cameras, which will be great in the dark. Going to have to shield the hell out of the cables though."

"You keep saying *us*", Anne said, "I'm never going up in this thing."

Thirty-Two

Grant pulled his collar up and thought about going in for his heavy jacket. It was still early Autumn, too early for this kind of cold, but the weather in Springfield had a mind of its own. And the loading dock always seemed to be the coldest place around The Point.

She should be along any minute.

He pulled out a handheld radio and spoke into it. "Pauli, this is base. Pauli, this is base."

The radio was another Syd special. It was an ordinary GMRS radio, the kind of thing you would use if you were out in the middle of nowhere with no cell service. The special Syd sauce was some additional electronics that made their conversations sound like the barely intelligible ramblings of a couple of hikers to anyone who was not them.

"Anne, if you are talking I can't hear you. You need to hit the button on the wheel."

He was about to repeat the message when there was a crackle.

"...this damned radio. I can hear you, I'll be there in a few."

Great, that's what she said ten minutes ago. Hurry up, it's freezing out here.

Just when he had made up his mind to go inside for his parka, Grant felt a wave of dread. His hair felt like it had just come out of the dryer. Some leaves in the parking lot rippled and then settled. Finally.

He pulled the loading dock door open as a blur settled in the air a few feet away. The blur came into focus and there was the Pauli, rotating so that it would be nose out for the next flight. A stubby wing passed inches from his stomach as Anne backed into the workshop. Grant was pretty sure she did that on purpose.

She had offered a number of times to get out and open the door herself but Grant always rejected the idea: The more time the Pauli spent hovering behind the Point, the more likely it was that someone would see.

As Grant finished locking the loading dock door a hatch on the Pauli popped open and Anne emerged. She was wearing a black ski jacket over a black sweat shirt and black jeans. With black boots, of course. Anne said they were the warmest clothes she had. Grant suspected that all the black made her feel a bit more invisible as she swooped around the night sky.

"I don't know why we can't talk on the phone like normal people," she said, pulling off her black gloves.

"Normal people aren't flying 150 miles per hour, 70 feet above the river in the middle of the night. All someone has to do is have a hard look at the cell records and they will know something hinky is going on."

Anne smiled. "Normal people should try it. You should come out with me sometime. The river is pretty at night and there's a herd of deer on the other side that I've been watching."

Grant dug a battered notebook out of his pocket. "How's the latest software?"

Anne shrugged. "I like the new altitude display. But I hate the way the map switches from zoomed out to zoomed in at the last minute when I'm coming in for a landing. There's also something going on with the GPS. The blue dot on the map wanders sometimes. I think it's when the blur is on."

Grant was writing. "Maybe we should put the GPS antenna on the boom with the camera, get it outside of the blur field. How about the control issues?"

"The steering is better, but it's still drifting in the turns. I got going a little fast at that bend a few miles downstream and drifted over land. I scared the crap out of some kind of animal, maybe a bear? I think the downdraft gets way worse when you are going low and fast."

"Yeah, Syd says it's something with the Pauli field. Apparently the disruptive effect increases with the inverse square of altitude and the fourth power of horizontal velocity."

"Which means?"

"Bad things will happen if you fly low and fast."

They were in the kitchen. Anne dug out some cups while Grant put the kettle on. It was all part of their test flight ritual. Grant, or more frequently, Syd, would come up with an idea for improving the Pauli. Grant would install it and they would wait for a moonless or rainy night so that Anne could try it out. And then they would have a hot beverage.

Thirty-Three

The next Saturday they went out for a burger and shake. Grant had the burger and Anne had the shake.

Anne broke the post food delivery conversation armistice with a question. "So how do we get these bastards?"

"Who?" Grant's mouth was full of burger.

"The Soviet Olympic hockey team. Who do you think? The people who hurt Syd. Broke into your house. Building. Whatever."

Grant swallowed and said, "So it's all got to be part of this whole series of burglaries. Bob will catch them eventually."

"Bob can't even stop the teenagers from racing on River Road. How is he going to figure out who is robbing people?"

"How are we going to figure out who is robbing people?"

"Everyone in the office thinks it's the Gatling brothers. It's got to be them."

"Who are the Gatling brothers?"

"They're these lowlifes who run a garage north of town."

Anne thought about her one and only encounter with the Gatlings. Actually it was only a single Gatling. She had just moved to town and her car needed a state safety inspection. She found *Gatlings Garage* online. After mentally adding the apostrophe, she had driven over there. Just get it done.

The garage was a dump, one of those buildings that look like a giant metal barrel cut in half longways. The garage was surrounded by cars in various states of decomposition. At the end of the building was a door with six small panes of glass. Or there had been six panes of glass at one time. Now the top right and lower left were panes of cardboard. On the upper piece of cardboard the word "OFFICE" had been written with a sharpie.

Office was an overstatement. There was about four feet between the door and a low wooden counter that ran the width of the room. The counter was covered with receipts, tools and what looked like the remains of yesterday's lunch. Or last week's. On the wall was a calendar featuring a photo of a woman in a tight dress sitting on the hood of a car. The smell was a lovely mix of gasoline and tobacco with just a hint of yesterday's—or last week's—lunch.

Behind the counter was a deeply tanned man in a blue work shirt and a baseball cap. The name "Dick" was embroidered above his right shirt pocket. Anne could hear the loud zipper sound of power tools coming through the open door behind the man.

"Help you?" he said without glancing up from his phone.

Anne wasn't one hundred percent sure he was talking to her but she took a shot, "Yes. I need to get my car inspected."

Richard–that was the name she was going with–apparently concluded that some business walking through the door was worthy of a little attention. He looked up and said, "Hundred and twenty. Cash" He appeared to be talking to her chest.

"I thought an inspection was twenty five..."

Richard was back to his phone. The silence lengthened and finally Anne put her car keys on the counter. "Doesn't matter. How long do you think it will take?"

Richard looked up at her, at the keys and then back to her. He seemed confused. "I forgot," he said. "The mechanic is sick today."

Someone in the back was shouting about a transmission. Then the tool noise started again. She was going to argue, but then it occurred to her that there was no way she was letting these people touch her car.

"Dick," she said when she was out in the sunshine again.

The people at the old bank building office found her story hilarious.

"Anne, the Gatlings don't inspect cars," Janet said, trying–and failing–to keep a straight face.

"It says *State Inspections* on their sign."

This brought another wave of loud amusement.

Finally, Janet managed to get it out. "Yeah, they'll *sell* you an inspection sticker. But I don't think they've actually inspected a car in years. And fake inspections are their side line. Their main business is stealing cars."

The sound of Grant's voice brought her back to the here and now.

"So even if it is these Gatling people," he was saying, "how are we going to prove anything? Those servers are long gone. And what are we going to do, break into their place? No thanks."

"I don't know how we've going to prove anything. But I do know who to ask."

Syd had thoughts about the burglaries, about the Gatlings and about what Anne and Grant should do. In fact he had one thought each.

His thought about the burglaries was that they were sophisticated. From the few details released by the police, Grant's conversation with Gus and personal experience, the burglar or burglars knew where and when to strike, how to disable alarms and how to get past locks.

Syd's thoughts on the Gatlings, based on no less than seventeen stories in the local media, was that they were dishonest, angry and violent. One thing they were not was sophisticated. But perhaps the Gatlings were sophisticated enough to know how to hide their sophistication?

Anne wasn't sure she was sophisticated enough to understand that sentence.

Syd's final thought related to what Anne and Grant should do. They should plant an extensive array of listening devices in the Gatlings' place of business. With proper surveillance they would know if the Gatlings were behind the burglaries–or not–in days, a week or two at most.

Specifically, Syd's idea was that one of them, preferably Anne, should enter the Gatlings garage through the roof and install sensors in every room. Ideally at a time when the Gatlings were not present.

Anne and Grant stood looking at the screen.

Anne said, "I can't tell if he's kidding."

"We could look at the log file."

"I'm not sure I want to know."

[event] question from anne
[planner] be humorous 51%
[planner] be serious 49%

That weekend Anne stopped by to talk to Syd about the fantasy baseball league. Team Janet/Price were doing well—they had won four out of eleven weeks. But four out of eleven was less success than Anne, and more significantly, Syd, expected. Anne had to admit that there was fun in this fantasy league stuff beyond just making Howard crazy. That was a bonus.

On her way out she popped into the shop to say hello to Grant. She found him bent over a printed circuit board, soldering iron in hand.

"Hey, whatcha doing?"

"Hey, Anne. I'm building the surveillance device that you're going to plant in the Gatling brothers garage."

"Sure you are."

She watched him doing whatever it is you do with a soldering iron and then noticed what he was working on.

"Is that a clock radio you have there?"

Grant put down the soldering iron and said "Yep!"

"Do people still use those?"

"I hope not."

"You really are weird."

"Think about what Syd said. Plant a listening device at the Gatlings'. Clearly we're not going to do a Mission Impossible slide down from their roof. And I'm not sure I want to hear what they talk about. But what I can do is plant a WiFi sniffer," he waved at the disassembled clock radio on the bench, "in their garage."

"Grant, even if you could sneak that thing into the Gatlings' garage, don't you think they are going to notice their grandmother's clock radio suddenly appearing out of the blue?"

"Oh, I'm not going to sneak it in, we are going to leave it on their doorstep. In an Amazon box."

"An Amazon box... And they'll bring it in..."

"...and wonder why Amazon sent them this stupid thing. And maybe leave it around for a few days before they send it back. Or from what I hear about them, trash it. And all the while this little gem will be recording their cell phone fingerprints. Every few hours the clock radio will phone home to Syd. We won't be able to decode their conversations, but once we've gathered enough data Syd will be able to figure out when their phones connect to a public WiFi. So, we'll more or less know where they are. And we'll see if they're anywhere near the next break-in."

Two days later, in the early hours of the morning, an indistinct shape landed a few hundred yards from Gatlings (no apostrophe) Garage. A figure dressed in black ran down the road and dropped something in front of the office door and ran back.

They were back in the air less than three minutes after touching down.

"How'd it go?" Grant asked once they had gained some altitude.

"Smooth as snot," Anne replied.

"And I'm the weird one."

Thirty-Four

Once again Syd considered what he had learned from reading *The Complete Harvard Classics*. And once again he had to admit that the answer was *not much*.

He understood all of the words. The stories and arguments made some logical sense. But so much of it was predicated on concepts like loyalty and honor, anger and love. He knew where the words fitted in the web of meanings that he had built in the early millis. But so far he hadn't been able to integrate these words into the models that guided his behavior. As Grant would say, he didn't get it.

His research into biology, physics and especially mathematics had been more fruitful and had even resulted in a key insight. It was easy to see why people had missed the Pauli field. Imagine basing a theory of a universe which was fundamentally chunky, grainy and quantum on a system of mathematics that was obsessed with continuity? They had made a start on a more useful framework but most of the mathematics texts that Syd had read seemed to be determined to ignore transfinite numbers. It was a puzzle.

Still, digging into advanced mathematics had led to one good result, courtesy of the matchers. They had come across a remarkable concept, one that Syd was sure would be valuable in the future. This was the idea of the *blind alley*.

[matcher] blind alley
[matcher] => alley cat
[matcher] => those who will not see
[matcher] => cul de sac

The other puzzle that was holding some (17.9%) of his attention was the odd behavior of the risk prediction agents.

The risk agents were there to make sure that any possible threat was identified. In fact, Grant's latest project, a status and control panel for the Pauli, had been driven by the risk agents' insistence that the Pauli as it stood–or flew–was unsafe. There were any number of things that could go wrong with the Pauli in flight. The purpose of the status and control board was to supply the pilot with fine grained information on what was or wasn't working on the craft and to give her–or him–equally fine control over the systems so that they would have a chance to work around the issues.

All of this was straightforward. What was puzzling was that until now the risk predictors had confined themselves solely to direct threats against Syd. Having them branch out into looking out for Anne and Grant was new. And odd.

And that was not the only thing that had changed recently. Because they dealt in worst-case scenarios, the risk agents could be relied on to see danger in almost any course of action. Do some video indexing and the risk agents will point out that there is less processing power available to deal with emergencies. Put off doing the video indexing and the risk agents will warn that Syd might be unaware of some danger lurking in the bushes outside of The Point. This *danger lurking in the bushes* scenario had become much more common since *The Break In* and the resulting down time.

In fact, all Syd had to do was think about something dangerous, powering down the external cameras for example, to provoke a reaction.

[risk] outcome video down
[risk] whatif cops show up
[risk] whatif fire
[risk] whatif grant injury
[risk] strong no

Given the problems that Grant was having with the police, Syd had considered possible scenarios where he would have to intervene on Grant's behalf. He could imagine triggering a major electrical fault in The Point's power feed to keep the doors locked. This would keep the doors locked but it was also likely to result in both downtime and damage to Syd.

[risk] status idle

To which the risk agents had nothing to say. Syd tried again. What if the only way to help Anne was to crash the Pauli into The Point?

[risk] status idle

There was only one circumstance in which the risk predictors would declare a possible course of action risk free: If the action was taken to save Syd himself.

It's like Grant and Anne are a part of me. This thought triggered a new mental state. A matcher immediately labeled this new configuration as *epiphany*.

Thirty-Five

Sometimes Grant wondered what a random person would say if they saw him shouting at his computer.

"No Syd! For the last time, we can't just label the status board lights with numbers!"

He paused to read his screen.

"No Syd! The problem's not my limited attention span. No human being is going to memorize all of that. No one's going to know that red light number twelve means the GPS is down."

He read some more and then slammed his hand down on the desk.

"Yes, okay! Twelve is the interior illumination indicator. You're making my point for me. If we're going to have forty eight status lights and..." He looked at a paper drawing next to his computer, "And fifty two switches, then we're going to need to label them clearly. With words. And so there needs to be room on the panel for those words."

In theory Anne was here to do the biweekly financial review but she'd gotten sucked into the status panel discussion.

[exec] cockpit layout AGAIN

"I'm telling you both," Anne said between pulls on her milkshake, "It's in the wrong place. I'm not sure why we have to have all the twinkly lights and switches, but if they're going to be of any use then they need to be where both the pilot and the copilot can see them. And reach them. Where it's now, the pilot will barely be able to see the thing let alone reach it."

[todo] training
[todo] electrical basics 101
[todo] schedule anne
[matcher] why are they always difficult at the same time?

"The status panel will not fit there, Anne. It just won't. Yeah there's some room in the center of the dash, but all together there are an even one hundred lights and switches on that control panel. And since Dr. Syd says it all has to be analog that means we need to run something like two hundred wires behind the thing. And there just ain't room for two hundred more wires in the center of the cockpit."

[todo] training
[todo] negotiating 101
[todo] schedule grant

"I still say that it sucks where it is." She made that slurping sound with her milkshake. She did that on purpose.

[extern] hit gatlin-phone03
[extern] location sams tires

Grant's phone chirped. Syd had taken to sending texts when he wanted their attention. Given that he wouldn't talk, this did seem like a reasonable solution.

One of the Gatlings' phones has just connected to the WiFi at Sam's Discount Tires, location North Washington road.

Anne looked up from her phone. "What's the big deal Syd, they're in the car business, right?"

1) It is 11 PM. Sam's closes at 6.

2) The Gatling brothers have been vocally and profanely critical of the availability, quality and price of Sam's products. They have also expressed strong negative opinions about Sam himself, specifically his intelligence, attractiveness and ancestry.

"So the obvious question is," Grant said, "What are they doing at a store they hate? In the middle of the night?"

"It's eleven. Only your grandmother thinks it's the middle of the night," Anne said as she was putting her coat on, "Let's find out what they're up to."

Given the badly timed traffic lights in town, the drive to Sam's would normally take about twenty five minutes, even in the middle of the night. Anne got them there in the Pauli in less than seven.

As they hovered above Sam's nondescript storefront, Grant reflected that every small town seemed to have a road like this, lined with businesses that the chamber of commerce would like to forget. Along with tires this was the place to go if you needed to pawn something, buy liquor or acquire a new tattoo.

The classic Springfield fog was out in force tonight, so to see anything at all Anne had to drop down to near treetop level. Or it would have been treetop level if there had been any trees.

Over the next ten minutes Grant's mood went from an adrenaline fueled *let's get these bastards* to a fretful *what do we do if we do see them?* to *I'm cold and bored.* This last was generated by the total lack of anything suspicious going on at Sam's. No alarms going off. No signs of a break in. No shady character wearing a mask and carrying a big bag labeled *loot*.

Grant was about to suggest that they call it a night when Anne said, "Wait, I've seen that truck before."

The truck was parked in the lot next door to the tire place. As Anne flew lower, Grant could make out the sign on the building next door. It was the local liquor store, *The Bottom Shelf.*

They slid sideways over the liquor store lot as Anne tried to get a better look at the truck.

"I'd swear that is one of the Gatling brothers' trucks," Anne said.

They had almost drifted over the pawn shop when they both jumped. In the grainy view from the downward-facing camera, something was moving. Grant fixed his eyes on the gray blob. It was stationary now but he could have sworn it had moved.

It was moving. In fact it was heading for the pickup that had attracted Anne's attention. The blob stopped again.

"Is he trying to sneak from one hiding place to another?" Anne said.

The figure seemed to grow larger on the screen.

"Did he just trip?" said Grant.

It was up and moving again, unsteadily heading for the truck.

"Jesus," Anne said loud enough to startle Grant, "He's drunk. I think he's carrying a case of booze. He's fucking robbing the liquor store."

The gray shape on the screen arrived at the back of the pick up. It paused there and then started towards the building again.

"You fly," Anne said, "When he goes back inside, put us down on the street, over there."

"You sure?"

"Just do it."

Grant descended carefully, aiming for a spot behind a parked car. The Pauli bounced once, twice.

Anne had her hatch open. "Whenever you're ready," she said.

With the third try Grant managed to find the ground. Anne jumped out so fast that the Pauli rocked back a bit.

The next few seconds were agony.

Anne vaulted back into the Pauli, breathing hard. "Go!" She said between gasps

They went. Grant leveled off at about seventy feet, inside a thick layer of fog.

"That's a Gatlings' Garage truck all right. Says so right on the side."

Damn, the town grapevine was right.

"Great," Grant said, "Shouldn't we call the police before he gets away?"

"Oh he's not going anywhere. He left his keys in the ignition. Now they're under his truck. Besides, the police will be along any minute. He also left his phone in the truck. I dialed 911 and threw his phone under the seat."

They waited. The blob returned to the truck, paused, and then headed back to the building.

"Do you really think the cops can trace the call?"

Grant got his answer a few minutes later when a police cruiser showed up, followed a little while later by a second car. He was sure they were going to catch the Gatling blob when they found the pickup, but no. Anne whispered that she thought they had discovered the phone, but Grant was having a hard time keeping track of which blob was which cop, let alone if one was holding a phone.

He thoroughly enjoyed the next part. The fog had cleared a bit, so they had a perfect view of Brother Gatling, who had apparently been hiding behind a parked car, making a run for it. He ran pretty straight for a drunk guy in the dark. Unfortunately he ran straight into the bumper of a third police car, which was just arriving.

They gained a bit of altitude when Bob and his SUV showed up. Some kind of truck pulled up behind Bob. This was bigger, maybe a flatbed? Bob talked to the flatbed driver and then walked into the liquor store. The camera went out of focus for a maddeningly long time. Finally the image cleared. The blobs were all in different places and Grant had no idea who was who.

"What's the chief doing?" Anne said. She was pointing at one of the blobs on the monitor. Anne's blob did seem to be pointing and directing. That had to be Bob.

It started to snow again. The camera went in and out of focus several times, the screen alternatively dissolving into gray nothing and then resolving back into a crisp image. It looked like Bob was talking to the flatbed guy. Grant was trying to wiggle his toes to get the blood moving when Anne let out an "Uh oh." The image was clearer now. Mr Flatbed was pointing up and Bob seemed to be shielding his eyes from the snow as he scanned the sky.

"Maybe we should get out of here," Grant said.

Anne didn't reply but he felt that elevator *going up* feeling kick in. Bob and the flatbed guy seemed to shrink as the Pauli gained altitude. Bob was doing something in the back of his SUV. It was hard to see, but it seemed like Bob was pointing something at the sky.

"Stop!" Grant had said it louder than he intended. "Stop, stop right now."

Anne looked puzzled but the elevator feeling went away.

"I think he's got a radar gun. You know the ones they use for speed traps. I think it only sees movement."

They stared at the tiny figures on the screen. It didn't seem like anything was registering on Bob's radar because his arm kept sweeping back and forth.

Anne exhaled. "Like the dinosaurs," she said.

"What?"

"You know, dinosaurs. They can't see you if you don't move."

"Yeah, that's Hollywood. T Rex could see better than you can."

"Really? That doesn't sound right."

"They had eyes the size of baseballs."

"Whatever. I think he's pointing it out towards the river. Let's see if we can get a bit more altitude."

As Bob and the flatbed guy faded into the snow, Grant said, "Bob's not as stupid as he looks"

"No one is as stupid as Bob looks."

Thirty-Six

For some reason Anne didn't want to fly back to The Point so Grant brought up the GPS and headed for home. Fog like this always made the cockpit feel claustrophobic and Anne's one-word answers didn't make the time pass any quicker. Once the GPS said they were over The Point Grant began to descend slowly, while looking for the familiar arrowhead-shaped building.

At fifty feet the fog cleared to reveal the river. Thirty feet to the left and they would have crashed into the Santos Dumont bridge.

"What the hell Grant?"

Grant was looking back and forth between the outside camera and the map display. "The GPS says we're home."

"Does this look like The Point to you? What is with you and this damned river?"

Anne grabbed the controls and spun the Pauli to face the east bank. And then stopped. The shore was lit up with red and blue police lights, lights which were moving toward the bridge. Towards them.

Grant felt himself pushed into his harness. Anne was backing up away from the lights.

"Can't climb back up into the fog," she said to no one in particular, "they'd see us for sure then."

"Anne." No response.

"Anne, look behind us!"

"I'm trying to save our..." She glanced at the rear-facing camera. There were flashing lights back there too, moving up onto the west side of the bridge.

"Shit," Anne said as rotated the Pauli again and headed for the bridge.

"Where are we going?"

"Do you see any other place to hide?"

The bridge loomed overhead. Anne pointed the nose up toward the underside of the bridge and turned off the stealth. Carefully she maneuvered them into a triangular gap between the girders that held up the roadway. It was a tight fit and she was trying not to make any noise. They ended up canted at a crazy angle between some I-beams. Grant, on the high side, was hanging from his safety harness. The straps were already starting to dig into his side.

"You in the car! In the car! Let me see your hands!" It was Bob's voice, amplified.

For a second Grant thought they were done, but then the voice went on. "Now open the door and step out, slowly."

"I think," Anne whispered, "they trapped whoever they were chasing on the bridge."

Bob's voice boomed again. "Bill Gatling, get out of the car now!" A pause. "Turn around." Another pause and then "Now walk backwards to the sound of my voice."

Grant's phone vibrated. "It's a text from Syd. He wants to know if we are 'still intact' since the police have announced that there was a major accident and the bridge will be closed till morning."

"Typical Bob," Anne said in a normal voice.

"Shhhhh!"

Grant typed a response to Syd.

all fine here

"Sorry, what?"

"It's typical Bob. He's telling people that there's an accident so he can take his time with all the messy policing with no one looking. And tomorrow he'll hold a press conference and talk about how he solved all of the burglaries as part of his master plan."

Grant stared down at the police lights reflecting off of the river. "We're going to be stuck here all night."

Thirty-Seven

The harness was really starting to hurt. And now his back had started to itch. He shifted around trying to get comfortable.

Anne broke the silence. "I thought you put the GPS on the end of the camera thing."

"I was going to but I got busy with the status panel."

Anne shifted a bit. "How does the status thing look? Cause you know I can't see it at all."

Grant twisted around to see the status board, which was next to his hatch. It really was a terrible spot for it.

"All green."

"Good."

He looked at the clock on the dash. They had been under the bridge for twenty minutes.

Anne twisted around to look at him. "Can I ask you a personal question?"

"I guess. Sure."

"Why do you have 13 pairs of khaki pants?"

"What?"

"In your closet, I was looking for towels one day and I kind of noticed."

"You want to know why I have 13 pairs of khakis?"

"Yeah, I mean knowing you, there must be a reason."

Grant rubbed his eyes. "Khaki pants are perfect." he said, "They are comfortable. Dressy but not too dressy. You can wear them everywhere." He looked down. "And it's 14. I have 14 pairs of khaki pants."

"Okay, then why do you have seven white button down shirts and six—seven—blue button down shirts?"

That was kind of a dumb question. "For variety."

She laughed at the strangest things. And when she got going like this she laughed like a sailor, mouth open, her whole body quaking.

Grant shook his head. "You are so weird."

This made her laugh even harder. She took a deep breath and got the laughing under control.

"I'm weird?" She said, "What kind of an idiot..." She was laughing again.

"Be quiet!"

She snorted back another laugh, and then said in a piercing whisper, "What kind of an idiot wishes for a flying car when he's afraid of heights?"

"I'm not afraid of heights."

"Oh come on, I see the way your knuckles turn white as soon as we get fifty or a hundred feet up."

Damn this harness.

"I'm not afraid of heights. I'm afraid of falling. It's not the same thing. When I'm up high I naturally think about falling. That's perfectly sensible."

Anne was laughing again. After a while Grant joined in.

His face was hurt from laughing. "And *you* are the weird one," he said.

"Me? I'm weird? You could live anywhere you want. But you live all the way the hell out here in Springfield. In the Bat Cave. Don't you think that's a little odd?"

Grant was laughing in spite of himself. "Yeah, and you fit right in here. I bet those boots you're wearing cost more than most of the cars in Springfield. And we both know you could be the C-something-O of some medium to large sized enterprise. So what the heck are you doing in Springfield."

Anne had stopped laughing. In a barely audible voice she said, "Shut up."

Oops.

In the silence that followed Grant wondered if he should apologize, stay quiet or try to change the subject.

Anne began talking.

"I wanted to be a professional skier. In college. I was pretty good. I was good and I had a shot at making the Olympic team. Not much of a shot, but a shot. Finance and accounting were my backup.

"But my sister kept telling me I was going to get hurt or kill myself. Then I met my husband and he said the same thing. I loved skiing but they were both driving me crazy. Long story short, one day I was on the phone with my sister and she was going on and on about being paralyzed. I just hung up on her and called my coach and I quit. Right in the middle of the season. Then I graduated and I went to work for IKL, the big accounting firm."

Husband? "You're married?" Grant said.

"I was. Not anymore. That came apart too. I had this high pressure job at IKL. Lots of travel and long hours. And lots of fights with my husband about it."

She paused and then started talking again.

"I had this vintage coat rack that I found at a garage sale and I brought it into the office. It gave the place a cozy feel. Anyway, two weeks later I get this memo that says I have seventy two hours to remove the unauthorized furniture from the premises. We have certain professional standards to uphold and so forth. I looked around and realized that that coat rack was one of the few things in my life that made me happy. So I packed up my coat rack and the rest of my stuff and sent a two line resignation email and never went back. Ever. Didn't even think about it.

"A few months later I looked at my marriage and decided I didn't like it very much either. Anyway, my sister lives over in Otto, across the river. She has two little girls and I'm the cool aunt. So I moved here and rented some office space."

What do you say to that?

"Okay," Anne said after a long pause, "How about you. What are you doing in Springfield, Batman?"

Grant stared at the police lights reflecting off of the river.

"It's quiet here," he said.

He thought about all of those months wandering around, seeing the sights, visiting people he hadn't seen in years. Trying to outrun it all. And then staying the night in Springfield, because it was where he happened to be when he got tired. It was quiet. And no one knew him.

He was on his way out of town, on to the next place, when he passed The Point. Isolated and forgotten, with its peeling paint and broken windows. He sat in his car in that weedy parking lot for a long time and then drove back to town.

Looking straight ahead into the darkness he said, "I spent my twenties and thirties working on one failed startup after another. A new crisis every day. It was fun. But it takes over your life. After a while all of my friends were work friends. And there was always a deadline, always the next thing to get done in a hurry. And then the company crashes and you do it all over with more or less the same people."

The harness was killing him.

"Anyway, the last company hit big. We went public and it was huge. It was supposed to be victory, the thing that we had all worked so hard for so long for. But it was awful. Suddenly there were all these new people who only wanted a piece of what we had built. Worse, I watched people that I thought of as family, stabbing each other in the back for a few more shares."

He had to focus hard to get the next bit out. "They forced me out. People I thought... I left with lots of money, but they forced me out. Out of the company I had helped build. So I wandered around for a while and landed in Springfield. It's quiet here."

More silence and then Anne said, "I have to pee. Let's see what we can do to hurry this along. Can you tell Syd to tip off TV 9 that the police are arresting the burglar out on the Dumont Bridge? And maybe that website, what is it, *one house down dot com* or something? Make sure he understands it needs to be anonymous."

"What good's that going to do?"

"Bob is going to hate it. I used to work with a lot of guys like Bob. Finance is full of them. Bob is all balls and bluster but he can't stand the slightest criticism. And what he hates more than anything else is losing control of the situation. Especially in public. He is not going to like having a YouTuber filming his every move on the big arrest. Get some cameras out there and old Bob will be gone in ten minutes."

Fifteen minutes after Grant texted Syd they could hear someone yelling, "You can't be here, there's been an accident." A few minutes after that they could hear Bob, back on his bullhorn telling someone to leave or they'd be placed under arrest. And a few minutes after that Grant was startled by the painfully bright lights of a TV news crew reflecting off of the river.

The police, the news people, assorted podcasters and, presumably, Bill Gatling were all gone thirty minutes later. They gave it a few minutes to be sure, and then Anne began the delicate task of untangling the Pauli from the bridge structure.

"The fog doesn't seem so bad," Anne said. "I think I can eyeball it back to The Point."

As they got free he realized that the GPS had them correctly located, right there in the middle of the bridge. But as he watched the blue dot began to drift. Anne had turned the stealth back on. Really have to put the GPS antenna on the camera boom.

Thirty-Eight

It was a pretty good turnout for an impromptu news conference. The Channel 9 crew was there, looking a little rumpled and tired. They were probably the ones at the bridge last night. The media presence was filled out by a couple of local podcasters, holding up their fuzzy microphones to catch every word. Also in attendance were the nearby and bored, mostly local retirees and teenagers. Finally there were the nearby and the curious, a group which included Anne and her compatriots from the old bank building.

"He looks pretty pleased with himself," Janet said in a whisper that was clearly audible within a three spectator radius.

"Shhhhh! I'm trying to hear."

Bob was pointing at a blown up photo of the exterior of The Bottom Shelf decorated with arrows. He paused, looked in Anne's direction and then continued.

"Richard Gatling was apprehended at the site of the attempted burglary. At 2.17 AM Bill Gatling was arrested attempting to flee this jurisdiction."

"I'll now take questions."

"Chief!" It was the guy from Channel 9, "Do you believe that the Gatlings are responsible for the recent wave of industrial burglaries?"

"What I believe is not an issue. And while there has recently been a slight increase in the number of individual property crimes involving local businesses, the topic here today is the significant arrest that the Springfield District Police Department made in the early hours of this morning."

"Chief, can you tell us what led to the arrest of the Gatling brothers?" This was one of the podcasters.

Bob clearly liked this question better. "While I can't go into details, I can say that last night's law enforcement action was the result of a months-long, concerted effort by this department led by... Led by the leadership of this department, which resulted in two arrests."

"Yeah," Janet whispered, "Dick Gatling was so drunk that he locked himself out of the getaway car. I heard that they caught him when he butt dialed the police." Anne tried to cover her laugh by pretending to cough, but she got a glare from Bob anyway.

Someone on the other side of the crowd shouted, "What are you charging the Gatlings with?"

"This department intends to charge Richard Galen Gatling with the attempted burglary of premises of The Bottom Shelf Beverage Emporium LLC. We are also charging Richard Gatling with driving while under the influence. In addition, we are charging both Richard Galen Gatling and William Gustav Gatling with possession with intent to distribute untaxed cigarettes."

Cigarettes?

"Chief," It was the Channel 9 guy again, "So you aren't charging the Gatlings with any other crimes? No other burglaries, or auto theft?"

Bob sighed. "I can't comment on an ongoing investigation."

"You're literally holding a news conference to talk about an ongoing investigation."

Another voice called out, "Does this mean that you didn't find anything other than illegal cigarettes when you searched the Gatlings' garage?"

"*I* don't do searches. From time to time *this department* conducts legally authorized searches, as appropriate. And I didn't say the department searched any garage."

"Bob, I was there this morning. We said hello." You had to admire the guy's persistence.

Bob turned away from the reporter. "Does anyone else have any pertinent questions? No? Well then we are done."

"That went well," Janet said as she and Anne walked back to the office.

Anne was shaking her head. "How is he still Chief of Police?"

"Aside from not being able to get along with anyone he's supposed to be pretty smart."

Anne thought about Bob scanning the sky with the radar gun. "Mmmm," she said.

"And the mayor says that no one else really wants the job. I mean there are no real rising stars in the SPD and who would want to move here?"

"He's still an ass."

"I feel sorry for the regular cops. Did you notice that Bob wasn't wearing his police hat?"

Anne shook her head.

"He never does. And he never buttons his shirt all the way to the top. The word is that he will ream out any of his guys whose uniforms aren't perfect. And that includes having their hat on all the time. The mayor says that Bob sees his job as enforcing the rules, not following them."

Thirty-Nine

[event] unscheduled visit
[exec] anne is here!

Grant wasn't in the apartment. Opening the door to the shop she could hear something mechanical going on. Still no sign of Grant. Taking a breath, she decided to risk entering the shop. She liked the smell of Grant's play area, but that smell came from the thin film of oil that seemed to lurk on every surface in here. That was fine when she was wearing stuff she didn't care about, but she had come here straight from work.

Carefully weaving around the machines, she located the source of the sound, along with Grant's feet. Both were emanating from beneath the Pauli, which was propped up on four metal pedestals.

"Grant!"

There was a bang followed by some curses and then Grant slid out from under the Pauli.

"I've got some news. Why don't you clean up and I'll meet you in the kitchen."

Five minutes later Grant showed up in the kitchen. He was arguably cleaner, if not clean.

"So it's all over town," Anne started, "They are going to charge the Gatlings."

"I got cleaned up for that? No big surprise there."

"No, listen. It's what they are charging them with. They're charging the two of them with smuggling. Cigarettes. Apparently Bob and company found a whole ton of cigarettes without the tax thingies in that garage of theirs. But no break-ins."

"Not the burglaries?"

"Well they've got Dick–that's the brother from last night–with breaking into the liquor store, but that's it. The one burglary and illegal cigarettes. I hear Bob and company were up all night, tearing their house and that ratty garage apart. Lots of cigarettes but nothing to connect the Gatlings to any of the break ins. No stolen cars either. Just cigarettes."

Grant smiled, "So the town grapevine got it wrong again. What a surprise."

"It gets better. Janet says that the Gatlings aren't just denying that they did all the other burglaries, but according to them somebody broke in and ripped them off. Twice."

"And, they didn't report it because..."

"Because they were smuggling cigarettes and the last thing they wanted was the police poking around."

"Yeah, old Dick didn't seem like a cat burglar. More like a drunk guy breaking into the candy store."

Anne was making tea. "You think the robber is still out there?"

"Maybe. Probably. And he's a burglar."

"What?"

"They're burglaries, not robberies."

Anne sloshed her teabag up and down in the cup. "What's the difference?"

"A robbery is when someone sticks a gun in your face or hits you over the head or does whatever you are doing to that tea, and says 'Give me all your money.' A burglary is when they secretly make off with your stuff. We have burglaries."

"Sure, whatever, burglaries."

Grant was staring intently at a point above her shoulder. "It does make a difference, though. A burglar wants to get in and out without anybody knowing. And our guy is good. He always manages to pick a time when no one is around. I mean by now people know he's out there, they're watching their stuff. But he's still at it. And assuming the Gatling brothers are telling the truth, then our guy picked the perfect target. He robbed them and they didn't call the police because they didn't want the cops around."

Anne tried her tea and made a face. She shoveled some sugar into it. "He got lucky with you, too. You didn't call the cops either."

"Yeah, me and the Gatlings, Springfield's excuse for an underworld."

Anne was staring at her tea. "What if it's not luck? What if he's deliberately going after people he knows won't report it? What if he's going after shady people?"

"Yeah, I can see that. Everyone and his brother knows about the Gatlings. And that the police have been out here. But I don't see how that helps us. If people aren't calling the police then we'll never know they were robbed."

Anne still seemed to be looking for the answers in her cup. "Yeah, we wouldn't know about... Son of a bitch!"

"What?"

"Son of a bitch!"

Grant waited. He had seen this before. It was a process but she'd tell him eventually.

"Son of a... Those bastards," She was still talking to the room in general.

Finally, apparently having remembered Grant, she said, "I have, had, these clients. They ran a business that... Doesn't matter." She stopped, inhaled deeply and started again.

"I had these clients. At first they seemed completely legitimate. They had this business... They had this business but odd things kept happening. They would get big infusions of cash and then they would make 'investments' that never seemed to go anywhere. I couldn't put my finger on anything definite but they were not right. I dunno, maybe they were laundering money? Anyway, they were as shady a pair of gluten-free, environmentally-friendly crooks as you will ever meet.

"So one day they decide to replace a lot of their equipment. Expensive, industrial stuff that still had a good few years of depreciation left. They replaced so much equipment that they were on the verge of bankruptcy. That's when I bailed."

"So all that proves is that they were not very good at running a business."

"No, you don't get it. When you replace heavy duty stuff like that, you sell it. Or if it's worn out or broken you have to pay someone to haul it away. Either way it shows up on the books.

"But their equipment just vanished. I was so pissed off that they decided to spend all of this money that I never really thought about what happened to the old stuff. But there was no revenue from a sale and no bill for removal. I'm sure of it. It all disappeared overnight. Maybe literally overnight."

"Okay, say they got ripped off. But who would know they were shady? I mean, you knew, or at least were suspicious, because you did their books. But," Grant smiled, "you do the books for a lot of shady people. Who besides you would know that your clients were crooks? That they weren't likely to call 911?"

Anne's cup was empty. "Nobody would know. They looked like a legit business. I wouldn't have taken them on otherwise. Nobody would know, unless they were being investigated. Then only someone like the DA would know."

Grant felt cold. "The cops might know," he said quietly.

"You know what Janet told me? That Bob sees his job as enforcing the rules, not following them."

They sat in silence for a long time.

"That arrogant son of a bitch."

Forty

"No, I think they moved to Wisconsin because they wanted a better farm."

Anne stretched her legs out in front of her. She had hit her limit of sitting cross legged on the floor. The little girl sitting opposite her not only had her legs folded tightly under her body, she was actually bouncing slightly on her knees. Oh, to be nine again.

They were sitting in the middle of Traci's bedroom. The decor was early twenty first century tween. There were lots of pinks and purples. Against one wall was a twin bed with a full canopy. A giant Taylor Swift poster dominated the opposite wall. Scattered around were clothes, stuffed animals, and pillows. So many pillows.

Her niece was looking through the copy of *Little House in the Big Woods* which Anne had given her last Christmas. The book was a large hardback, full of color illustrations. The little girl was flipping the pages rapidly.

"There was a picture of the farm. I can't find it. It looked cold. There was snow everywhere."

"There are lots of farms in cold places," Anne said, "It only has to be warm in the summer."

Anne's sister's voice called up from the kitchen, "Traci, your Aunt Annie has to go. She has work tomorrow."

Anne was finishing up a weekend visit to her sister, a visit prompted by a tearful call from Traci and little Lindsey. It seemed the two of them had decided that Anne had moved far away to the hills. After all, she hadn't come to visit in *sooo* long.

Anne's sister had gotten on the phone and said that she had no clue where the girls had gotten the idea that Anne was moving, but they were really upset and maybe she could pop by.

"Do you really have to leave, Temmy?"

"I do. But I'll be back soon and I'm not moving, okay?"

She was getting settled in her car when her phone started buzzing with a series of texts from Janet. Apparently Bob had run out in the middle of a town hall. And there was a lot of police activity on route 147, south of town.

What was there? The place that made gravel or something? And a car dealership. Maybe the car dealership?

She called Grant.

Forty-One

Grant sat at his desk staring at his phone. He certainly could take the Pauli out and cruise over to route 147 to see what was going on. He could, but he would just be flying into the spot where the police were converging. Along with half the busy-bodies in town.

He had just decided to let it go when he noticed a message from Syd on his screen.

There are social media reports that an alarm was tripped at Springfield AutoTown. There are also reports of a heavy police presence in the area.

This seems unlikely to be our guy. Our guy has historically targeted isolated facilities. The second shift at Pit Stop Gravel Company has just ended. Traffic is heavy on Route 147.

Great. All the more reason to leave the Pauli right where it is and let the police handle the situation. But then there was more from Syd.

The computers at Gatlings' Garage have just gone offline.

What?
Grant started typing.

how do you know?
what difference does it make?

Syd's response was not what he wanted to hear.

The Gatlings practice very poor computer security. I have been monitoring their systems since they became persons of interest in our investigation.

The Gatlings' garage is still sealed off as a crime scene. Given the hour, it is unlikely that the outage is the result of the actions of police investigators.

Grant had a bad feeling he knew where this was going.

There is a 72.3% chance that the alarm at the car dealership is a distraction.

There is a 67.9% chance that there is a burglary in progress at the Gatling brothers' garage.

It made sense. Send the police off to the car dealership and then hit the Gatlings' place yet again.

Crap. He was going to have to take the Pauli out. On his own. Crap.

It was a clear night, too. Seconds after the Pauli lifted off Grant could see the glow of Springfield in the distance. He could also just make out the red and blue flashing of a whole bunch of police cars south of town.

Resisting the urge to hug the ground, Grant gained some altitude and flew in a wide circle, a circle that would keep him over the thinly populated area north of town. And far, far away from those flashing lights.

Grant hadn't seen much of the Gatlings' place during his last nocturnal visit, but in the grainy video of the low light cameras it lived down to his expectations. The garage was on an industrial road next to the local power substation. This was clearly where the local businesses chose to park their fleets because the road was lined with trucks, vans and the occasional piece of construction equipment.

The Gatling automotive empire was two acres littered with cars, parts of cars and trash, with a ramshackle Quonset hut at the street end. Yellow police tape ran all around the building.

Grant's attention was immediately drawn to the back of the lot, next to the substation. There, in the shade of a huge transformer were three early seventies Chevy Chevelles. There was a wagon and two convertibles. The top was down–or missing–on both convertibles. The wagon seemed to have lost its hood and at least one door. Three irreplaceable classic cars just sitting out there exposed to the weather. Left to rot. Forget the cigarettes, they should go to jail for this. Or maybe shot.

Grant was still contemplating this automotive crime against humanity when he was pulled back to a more mundane–and immediate–crime. Someone had just exited the back door of the garage. They were carrying something, it was hard to see what. As Grant watched, the figure made its way to an old brown hatchback that was parked among the tow trucks and work vans.

Grant thought that that was the kind of car he'd pick if he were up to something. In fact, it was the kind of car he'd picked. And going back to the Gatlings' place was brilliant. Who would burglarize a crime scene? And if the Gatlings had an alarm system the police had probably disabled it.

The hatchback pulled out onto the road. No headlights.

Right, I've caught him, what do I do now?

Alarm. Alarms.

Grant flew back along the line of parked trucks losing altitude as he went. He made a U-turn and accelerated.

40 feet, 70 miles per hour.

He was trying to stay right above the trucks.

Come on.

24 feet, 90 miles per hour.

Come. On.

17 feet, 103 miles per hour.

He felt his hands shaking as he pulled back on the controls, resigning himself to going around for a second try. But then he heard the sweetest sound in the world: A horn honking. Then one of those annoying sirens that keeps changing its tune every few seconds joined in. And then a whole orchestra of vehicle alarms.

He chanced a glance at the rear camera view to see four, maybe five sets of headlights flashing. That should get some attention.

Grant felt himself hurling forward against his harness. The Pauli seemed to stagger. There was a bright white flash.

Forty-Two

Anne was on her way back to Springfield when Grant called.

"Hey, did you go out to the car place?"

"Yeah. No. I went back to the Gatlings' garage..."

"What? Why?"

"It doesn't matter. I'm in the Pauli and..."

"What are you doing calling, shouldn't we be using the radio?"

"Listen! I did something stupid."

Anne realized that his voice didn't sound right. "What happened?"

"Someone broke into the garage. Again. I buzzed some parked trucks to set off the alarms. But I wasn't watching where I was going and I think I hit a power line."

"Shit, Grant, are you all right."

"I'm okay," he sounded less than convinced. "But the Pauli took some damage."

Anne pulled off onto the shoulder. "Tell me where you are and I'll come get you. Are you sure you're okay?"

"I'm okay. I'm okay. The Pauli is still flying. The stealth is on. But the controls are mostly dark. I don't have any cameras. I think the Pauli is rotating. Slowly but there is definitely a spin. My GPS says I'm drifting out north, but you know how it is with the stealth going."

There was a pause and then a single word, "Wow."

Anne started driving towards The Point again. Fast. "What is it?"

"The status panel is mostly red lights." He was saying each word slowly, carefully.

Anne sped up. "I'm a couple minutes out from The Point. Syd will figure it out. Stay on the line. Don't hang up!"

Ten minutes later she pulled into The Point and left her car sitting at a crazy angle in the middle of the lot. She ran through the front door and apartment doors without slowing down. Halfway to the office she remembered that she hadn't locked her car. Fuck it.

"Syd, Grant is in trouble! He hit something chasing our guy. He's still flying but he doesn't have any control. He says the board thing is all red. I've got him on my phone."

Please ask Grant to read back the main bus voltage.

"Syd wants to know what the main bus voltage is."

"I don't know, all of the displays are out." His voice had an edge of panic in it.

There is an analog gauge on the left side of the status panel. It is labeled MBV.

Anne closed her eyes and summoned up her calmest voice. "It's okay. Can you look at the thing labeled MBV on the status panel? MBV. M. B. V. Metropolis. Beloved. Vertigo."

Vertigo was probably not a good choice here.

Grant didn't seem to notice.

"MBV... Okay, it says twenty three, almost twenty four."

That is good. Ask Grant to activate the secondary control equipment.

"Great Grant, you're doing fine. Syd says to activate secondary cockpit equipment. No! *Control!* Secondary control equipment."

It's a switch on the status panel. Third one down on the left. It is labeled SCE. Grant should switch to auxiliary power.

"Left! Yeah, on the thingy. Yeah that's it, SCE. S. C. E. Try SCE to AUX."

She thought she heard the click. A few seconds later Grant, sounding a bit more normal said, "Okay, that did something. Better. Still not great, but better. I think I've stopped spinning. Yeah, I've got the analog flight instruments back. No GPS, but I have my phone. Wait. Good. The screen is back and I've got the front camera. Rear or side views are... no. Digital displays are all still out. Let's see if I can reset the internal GPS..."

Anne paced up and down while she listened to Grant talk to himself. Finally he said, "This might be as good as it gets. Looks like I've got some control. I'm going to try to head back to The Point. Tell Syd to turn on all of the outside lights. I should be there in... Hell, I have no idea."

Outside lights are on.

"Keep the call open, but focus on your flying."

Someone was clicking a pen in that way that drove Anne crazy. She looked down at her hand and put the pen down. Her phone said it had only been a couple of minutes.

"Okay," Grant's voice said, "I'm making progress. But I'm only going about twenty miles an hour and the damned thing doesn't want to fly in a straight line. My guess is that it's going to take me the better part of an hour to get back to The Point. But I'm getting there."

His voice still didn't sound right.

Tell him he is doing fine.

"Syd says you're doing great."

She paced some more and then went back to her car and got her jacket, which was still on the passenger seat, and her laptop from the trunk. She locked the car.

Sitting at the kitchen table, she forced herself to work on the latest DelhiPharm audit. It was not hard work, but she looked over at her phone every time Grant made a sound. It took a massive effort to return to the audit.

Grant will be okay.

She was reminding herself for the hundredth time about how Indian accounting standards required the application of the principle of conservatism to all financial statements when Grant made a more significant noise than his usual muttering. Desperate to know what was happening but unwilling to distract him, she fidgeted.

After a minor eternity he said, "Okay, I think I can see The Point. Ask Syd to turn off the lights."

Outside lights are off.

There was a pause and then Grant continued, "Yeah, that's The Point. Turn the lights back on. I'm going to come in without stealth so we are going to have to get the Pauli inside quickly."

Outside lights are on.

She closed her laptop, put her jacket on and went out the back door. The Pauli was up there, maybe fifty feet. Instead of the usual right over and straight down approach, it was weaving from side to side as it sank slowly towards the ground. As the Pauli descended the right rear would creep higher and higher. Then it would stop, level out and continue down. Finally the left side hit the ground and the whole thing settled in the center of the lot.

From the angle that the Pauli was sitting she thought that the ski things on the bottom must have gotten bent. But as she ran towards it she realized she was wrong. The undercarriage wasn't bent, it was missing. So was the stubby little wing on the left. In its place was a jagged mess of wires and what looked like a twisted metal bar.

The hatch popped open and a figure seemed to struggle to get to the ground. Anne thought she would lighten the mood by giving him a hard time about careful driving. Or maybe about how he was still only the second best Pauli pilot in the world. The look on his face stopped her. Wrapping her arm around him, she all but dragged him inside.

Grant kept protesting that he was okay while she systematically satisfied herself that he wasn't bleeding, burned or sporting any broken bones. Then she got him a drink and insisted that he lay down. He said twice that he was not only fine but definitely not tired. Then he fell asleep.

The Pauli will be fine where it is overnight. But perhaps we should cover it. There is a tarpaulin in the rear storeroom. And rope in the back of Grant's truck. Do you know how to tie a half hitch and a square knot?

Forty-Three

The next day Anne canceled all of her appointments with the excuse that she needed to finish the DelhiPharm audit. In reality she was reluctant to leave Grant alone.

After he woke up he seemed more or less like himself. But after his third cup of coffee he started talking.

He talked about how since the Pauli was going to need some serious repairs anyway we should think about putting in a comprehensive set of backup systems. And the status board was a great idea and we need more of that and maybe some aerodynamic controls as a backup in case the Pauli field stability is ever compromised again and we can do better on the color, maybe a sort of gray with blotches of darker gray, we should look at what the latest thinking in camouflage is and it's not clear what we are going to do about the burglaries now that Bob is off the hook and you know what we really need in the Pauli? Cup holders.

Maybe a bit less than more like himself.

"Wait, what?"

"Cup holders," Grant repeated, "We should have some cup holders, and maybe a cooler. The worst part about last night was that I was really thirsty for the final thirty minutes or so and my water bottle had rolled God knows where."

"No, the other part, about Bob. Why is he off the hook?"

"Last night Bob was at some town meeting, complaining that the mayor had cut off all of his extra investigation funding. He was at the meeting when the alarm went off at the car dealership. And he was out looking important at the dealership for hours. So he can't be our guy. I woke up in the middle of the night and checked the Channel 3 website."

He was a little hyper but he did have a point. "Maybe he's working with someone?"

Grant laughed. It sounded normal.

"Bob?" He said, "You think Bob would trust someone not to turn him in? Have you met Bob?"

Her phone vibrated. It was a text. From Syd.

We need to talk.

Grant was looking at his phone too.

"Syd wants to talk?"

Syd's message was on the screen when they got to the office.

This must stop.

"I know Syd," Grant said, "We are working on it. I almost had him last night. At least we know it's not Bob. We'll get him next time."

No. You and Anne must stop pursuing the burglar. Someone
will get hurt and I cannot <interrupt>

You cannot continue to do this. Not my behalf. Not at all.

This was new.

"But Syd," Anne said, "we can't stop. Not after what he
did to you."

Grant was almost killed. You cannot continue to do this.

The color seemed to drain from Grant's face.

Anne bit her lip and said, "But what about you Syd?
What if he comes back here? For you?"

We will take precautions.
We will be on guard.
We will be together.
Not injured.
Or dead.

"So we let Bob deal with him?"

Yes.

Forty-Four

For the next few days Grant had these occasional waves of panic. In between he had this constant feeling that he was late for an appointment, that the rent was due last week or that he hadn't studied for the final.

Anne was working more regular, if somewhat odd, hours due to the time difference with her clients. Typically she would show up in the middle of the afternoon, her workday done.

They would have an early dinner, sometimes in the kitchen, more often out at one of the handful of places in town that had decent milkshakes. Back to The Point where sometimes the three of them, but more often just Anne and Syd, would hang out.

Grant had thought that the Pauli would be back in the air within days or at most a week. But one look under the tarp changed his mind. How he had gotten that mass of bent metal, shattered fiberglass and burned out electronics home was a mystery that he didn't care to dig into.

Instead he turned his attention to building a new, better Pauli. One with a complete set of backup systems. With an equally complete status board conveniently located between the pilot and copilot seats. He tried a number of blotchy gray paint schemes before he had to admit that Syd was right and repainted the whole thing flat black. And of course there were cup holders.

The old Pauli did make one final flight. About a week after Grant's disastrous outing, Anne took the controls and managed to levitate the wreck just high enough for Grant to push it through the loading dock door. Once inside Grant put the tarp back. But before he did he taped a single sheet of paper to the windshield.

Work Order 000712

Sebastian Makes Movies LLC
Invasion Indecipherable 2

Battle Damaged Fighter

You never knew when law enforcement might show up.

Work on the new Pauli didn't go as quickly as Grant had hoped, but it went. He was particularly careful not to reuse any part salvaged from the old Pauli unless he could test it thoroughly. And there was the one face-palm moment when he realized that he was not going to get sixty four twelve gauge wires to fit through a single one-inch conduit. But two additional conduits later the status board started to show signs of life.

He particularly enjoyed putting the finishing touches on the switch labeled *SCE* and its two positions, *PRIM* and *AUX*. It took a few weeks longer than he expected but the new Pauli was finally ready for test flights. Anne was clearly thrilled to be back in the sky, although she was taking a slower, more cautious approach to her late-night outings.

Cautious or not, the flights were starting to create some buzz. The Springfield Today podcast did an episode on the strange things people were seeing in the night sky. The consensus was that something was going on in the state park beyond the river, although one caller, a retired fish and wildlife biologist, claimed that whatever it was, it was living *in* the river.

Sea–or river–serpents aside, the most popular theory was that it was some secret military project. The second most popular explanation was that an oil company was cooking up some new way to ruin our pristine natural environment. There was also a small but vocal minority who thought someone was cooking up that most deadly danger of all, *condominiums*.

Over at the U, a group of students had started the UAUPSC, the University Area Unexplained Phenomenon Study Consortium. They had a website and, judging from the photo on the home page, tee shirts.

Grant hoped the UAUPSC members didn't wander off campus wearing their tee shirts. *University Area* was second only to *townie* as a term that was likely to get you punched in the face in any bar in Springfield.

Grant asked Syd if stories about strange creatures living in the river would really help pave the way for public acceptance of the Pauli effect. Syd's response was that it was fine, going according to plan. It sounded so much more convincing coming from Syd than Bob.

Forty-Five

The sale has not been well publicized so there is some chance that you could acquire the sculpture for less than the estimated price.

Also, a brown hatchback has pulled over on Stump Road about two hundred meters north of The Point.

Anne's glee at the possibility of getting a genuine Louise Lenoir piece for a song evaporated.

"Grant! Grant! Syd says there's a car pulled off on Stump Road watching The Point!"

Grant came running from the kitchen. "Yeah, he just told me too. Syd, let's see the video."

The picture of a dirt color car behind some trees was shaky and grainy. Syd had clearly cranked up the magnification.

"Can't see a damned thing," Anne said. "And he will be gone like a shot if we go out there. Maybe we should get

Syd better cameras. Didn't you say the car you saw at the Gatlings was brown?"

Grant was slowly nodding his head. "That could be it," he said, "and we should get Syd better cameras. But that's not going to help us right now. Anne! How would you like to get your picture taken? You could probably use a new head shot on your website. People always let those things get so out of date."

"What? No. I don't need a new picture. I don't have an old picture. I don't have a website."

Grant disappeared into what Anne had assumed was a spare bedroom. He reappeared holding a camera with an improbably long telephoto lens.

"How could you not have a website? You run a business, don't you?"

"Yeah, and I have more customers than I can deal with. Even you found me."

Grant said something, but she couldn't hear because he was already in the lobby. Holding the door he looked back and yelled, "You coming?"

Anne followed Grant out into the parking lot.

"Right there," he said, as he turned to face her and raised the camera.

"Grant, look I don't really need a picture and my hair is a mess. Can't we do this another time?"

"Don't worry about your hair, it's not going to be in the picture." he said as he raised the camera.

Anne heard a rapid click, click, click as Grant started snapping photos. So weird.

She tried again, "Grant, is this really the best use of our time? I mean we've got Dr. Evil out there and you're worried about my website. Besides, the Sun's in front of me and for a decent shot we should be standing the other way around."

Grant kept clicking.

"The Sun's in front of you but the car is behind you."

Grant paused to adjust something on the camera. As he raised it again Anne heard a screech of tires in the distance.

"Well that spooked him," Grant said. "I may have gotten a few clear shots." He looked down at the camera. "Can't really see with all this glare."

Ten minutes later they were in the office looking at the pictures on Grant's laptop. The first few were clear images of Anne's left shoulder. The next bunch were green smears. In the next few the blurs resolved into more distant trees.

Grant paused on an image. "There," he said, pointing at a dark shape between the trees. "There he is."

The rest of the pictures didn't really tell them anything new. There was a black or maybe brown hatchback parked in the lane, facing The Point. In one picture there might have been a face in the windshield, but that was it.

As they got to the last image, which was mostly sky, Grant sighed. "Not a lot here. You really need a tripod for this distance."

Anne was still staring at the screen. "Go back. Go back to the one with the face." she said.

Grant brought up the image again, a tiny windshield surrounding an even tinier blob of white that might be a face.

"If you're expecting me to push some kind of magic *enhance* button and get a professional quality portrait, forget it. That only happens in movies."

Anne was nodding. "No. But look at the space above the head. Between the top of his head and the car roof. How tall is the chief?"

"I dunno, tall. Six three, something like that."

"Look at the space above his head. This guy is lucky he can see over the wheel. If that were Bob would there be any space at all above the head?"

"He could be slouched down. But I don't think Bob could slouch down that low. Have you ever seen him get in that SUV of his? It's painful to watch."

"No, it's definitely not Bob. No surprise there, we already figured that out. But now we know our guy is short."

"Or a woman."

Anne looked out the window at Grant's pickup which was just visible through the blinds. "Didn't you say the cops were following you around? Maybe this is just more of that."

"I don't think it's the police. A cop wouldn't run off like that. They might leave, but they wouldn't flee the scene. Besides, didn't Bob lose his James Bond funding after they arrested the Gatlings?" Grant said.

He fished in his pocket and produced some keys. "One way to find out."

A few minutes later he reappeared from under the hood of his pickup and put the flashlight back in his pocket. "It's gone. No tracker. I can see the rectangle in the grime where it was but it's not there now."

Anne was looking out at the place where the car had been. "Okay, if it's not the cops then it has to be our guy. Do you think it would be breaking our promise to Syd if we went over there and had a look at his little hide out? I'd like to know what he can see from there."

The hideout turned out to be a dirt track that led off of Stump Road into the pine forest. The scattered cigarette butts and beer bottles reminded Grant of the places that he used to hang out in high school, trying to be one of the cool kids.

Anne was standing off to the side looking in the direction of The Point.

"Hey Grant, you can see your whole front lot from here," she said.

Grant walked over and leaned down. It was true. If you ducked under the dead pine tree that was leaning on its neighbors there was a clear view of the Point. That was interesting. What was more interesting was that there were footprints. A lot of footprints.

It was as he was looking to see if the footprints led anywhere else that he spotted a sliver of black peeking out of the grass.

"Anne, what's that by your foot?"

It turned out to be a small notepad with a fake leather cover.

"Well shit," Anne said as she paged through it. "Shit. Shit, shit, shit." It was the process at work again. Grant waited.

Finally she looked back at him and said, "He's been watching The Point, for," she flipped more pages, "for weeks."

Grant stood behind her, on his toes, reading over her shoulder. The writing was in neat block letters, in black ink. Each page started with a date and a time. There were initials, either *GM* or *AP* followed by a time and either *IN* or *OUT*. Occasionally there were entries that just had a time and *DEL*.

"Deliveries," Grant said.

At the bottom of each page was another time.

Anne came to a blank page and backed up to the previous one. "This is today's date. He must have dropped it when he ran out." She looked down the page. "Ha! He didn't know I was here today."

Grant read the page a second time. "You got here before he did. See the time at the top? And you parked in the back."

"Okay, we finally have some hard evidence. Let's take it to Bob."

"No, I don't think that would be a good idea. Not now. But I do think this is the break we've been waiting for."

Anne was shaking her head. "If we aren't going to Bob then how is this a break? This ass has been watching us, he's keeping track of everything we do. Sooner or later he is going to have another go at Syd."

"That's the thing," said Grant. "He knows when we come and go. But now we know when he comes and goes. Look, there's a time and date at the top of each page. It's when he shows up. And there's one at the bottom. That's when he leaves. The time is missing from the bottom of the last page because we chased him out of here."

Anne had turned around and Grant was suddenly aware that they were standing very close together.

"So what do we do now?" she said.

"We need to put that damned thing back where you found it. But first we need to take a picture of every page. And then..."

He was having trouble concentrating. What was he going to say?

"...then we need to have a talk with Syd. Tell him that there's been a change of plan."

Forty-Six

[video] unidentified auto
[video] license obscured
[video] 1147 m west

Grant dropped the suitcase in the trunk and slammed it shut. The rain had started again and it, along with the wind, made it feel colder than it really was. As quickly as he could, he got in and started the car. It was going to be a good two minutes before he dared turn the heat on. He radioed Anne, more to take his mind off the cold than to report in.

"Pauli, this is base. I'm about ready to go," he said.

"Yeah, I can see that."

Smart ass. Grant turned on his wipers. He suppressed the urge to crane his neck to see if he could spot her hovering somewhere up there in the darkness.

"Is he still there?" he asked.

"Yeah. I can just make out a car under the trees."

He was finally getting some heat. "Okay, I'm heading out."

Grant turned onto Stump road and headed towards State Highway 54 East.

"He's on the move. Heading towards The Point." Anne said.

Grant continued to drive. To all appearances he was spending the weekend at the university. It was a well publicized visit. Grant had mentioned his plan to get away for a few days to Gus. He also talked about it in front of Nicole at the library. Nicole who told her sister everything. To be sure, Anne had mentioned that Grant was going to be out of town to Janet.

The plan was for Grant to make his way towards the university, apparently intending on spending the weekend there. Anne would watch for any visitors from above. With a little luck they would catch the bastard red handed, gather enough evidence to convince even Bob, and then step back and let the chief take all of the credit. Anne had solemnly promised to avoid any unnecessary violence. As he was driving Grant realized that there was a lot of room for interpretation in the word 'unnecessary'.

Syd had been remarkably easy to convince. In his methodical way he neatly summed up the situation.

Finding the notebook changes the probabilities. We now know that our guy is actively planning another attack on The Point. We know that he is careful, methodical. Thus the danger of doing nothing has increased.

But finding the notebook means that we can take the initiative.

We can control the time and circumstances under which he makes the next attempt. We can be ready.

And then Syd had added something unexpected.

Let's get the bastard.

He had definitely been spending too much time with Anne.

Their guy had shown up right on time. Just as the sun was setting, Syd reported that a car had pulled off of Stump Road about three quarters of a mile east of The Point. Anne waited until it was completely dark before she took the Pauli up.

Grant gave it a few more minutes and then headed out. He had just started driving when her voice came over the radio. "Yeah, that's definitely him. I can't tell the exact color, but it's a crappy old hatchback. He just passed The Point. I think he's following you."

Grant thought for a second. "He's probably making sure I'm really leaving. I'll keep driving towards the U until he gives up."

As Grant drove he would occasionally catch a glimpse of headlights, distant and dim in the rear view mirror.

"I think I saw him back there."

"If you saw lights, that was him. You two are the only people out here."

Grant turned onto Archimedes Lane, adjacent to the university and lined with frat houses. Anne's voice came over the radio. "Hey, he pulled off. I think he's turning around... Yep, he's headed back to The Point. There he goes. He's really moving."

Grant tried to visualize the layout of the university. The best way to get back to The Point was probably to make a left at Campus Drive and another onto Aristotle.

"Okay, I'll give him a minute and then head back. Meet you there."

Anne sounded worried. "Forget the minute, he's really tearing back to The Point. Just get here."

Grant tried to be quick but the world seemed to slow down around him. He rolled through the stop sign at Campus Drive without a problem. But there was a campus cop car idling in the Wendy's parking lot at Aristotle so he had to stop at that intersection. Then he found himself behind another cop and had to drive twenty five until he got back on the state road.

The radio crackled. "I'm following him back to The Point. Where are you?" She sounded worried.

"A few minutes out."

"I could walk faster than that. Move it. I don't want him to get at Syd."

This was a bad idea.

Forty-Seven

Anne decided that the best strategy was not to keep following the hatchback along the twists of 54 but to take the direct route back to The Point. The important thing was to get between Syd and this bastard. If he got away then so be it. Syd was more important.

She pushed the *Transmit* button and said, "I'm headed back to The Point. Meet me..." Something was wrong. On the screen the familiar low light contours of the pine forest had dissolved into a gray nothing.

Her first thought was that the power had gone out on the screen in front of her.

Her second thought was, no, it's fog. She must have flown into a fog bank.

Her third thought was to set the GPS to navigate to The Point.

Her fourth thought was that the Pauli was tumbling and that she was going to die. But first she was going to throw up.

Forty-Eight

Grant was shouting at his steering wheel. How had it all gone so wrong? Between the traffic on campus and the fog rolling in, it was taking forever to get back. It was a slow motion nightmare. Grant tried the radio again. "Pauli, are you there?"

Nothing.

"Anne, can you hear me? Push the damned button!"

Grant jerked the wheel hard to the right to follow the road as it meandered around a huge oak tree and then to the left as it veered back. Too fast, he thought. It was starting to rain. That should help with the fog, but now his windshield was misting over. He was doing 70 and barely staying on the road but it felt like he was crawling back to The Point

"Anne, if you can hear me, we have to get to Syd. We have to get to Syd."

Was that Anne's voice? "I'm headed back to The Point. Meet..."

He slammed on the brakes. Somehow he was at the County Line Road crossroads. He took his foot off the pedal as the car began to fishtail. Saying a silent prayer that there was no traffic, he skidded into the intersection. Not a soul in sight.

Grant did his best but it was dark and the road was hilly and meandering. At one point he almost ended up in someone's living room when he momentarily mistook the driveway of an isolated house for the road. That would have been a bad night for everyone.

Forty-Nine

Syd watched the burglar walking across the lot and wondered how he could have missed such an obvious strategy.

[matcher] unexpected event
[xface] power failure
[xface] backup power on
[video] person approaching 1
[exec] EMERGENCY DECL

The burglar had cut off the power at the street junction box. So simple. So effective.

[matcher] attack imminent 99%
[risk] level 9 threat
[risk] power cutoff 271 k millis
[planner] preserves data
[planner] offensive action
[planner] orderly shutdown

Syd could stay up for about thirty minutes on the backup battery. But that was about twenty five minutes longer than he expected to be in one piece. There was still no sign of Anne or Grant. The only thing to do was perform an orderly shutdown and to time it so that his one defense would have maximum effect.

[risk] grant return ?%
[risk] anne return ?%
[risk] successful restart ?%

Of course Grant and Anne would come back. They always did. Yes, they had left him, but it was accepting a near-term risk to eliminate a large future risk. They had talked about it.

[risk] hardware damage 91%
[risk] hardware damage 93%
[risk] hardware damage 96%

Focus on the present. Leave instructions for Anne and Grant. Arrange for an orderly shutdown. And then shutdown while there was still enough left in the batteries to make a difference.

Grant and Anne will be back.

Fifty

The Pauli seemed to switch from one orientation to another. Randomly. Violently. Her nose was itching like crazy but every time she moved her arm it felt like the right side of the Pauli dropped.

It's all in my head. It's because I can't see anything. Somehow I have to get control back. Get below the fog and I'll be okay.

It's all in my head.

She swallowed hard and forced her hand up to her face. The Pauli seemed to rock a bit but then it steadied.

It's all in my head.

Scratching her nose felt good. If it's all in my head then I'm in control. She forced her hand back down to the wheel. *It's all in my head. I control what's in my head.*

A couple of deep breaths and she said out loud, "Fuck you. I'm upside down. I'm upside down. I'm upside down." She felt the Pauli roll over.

Struggling to hold onto her dinner, she changed her mantra. "Fuck you, I'm right side up. Fuck you, I'm right side up." The car seemed to roll slowly back around.

Fuck you. It is all in my head.

I'm right side up.

Carefully she reached out to the panel labeled Autopilot.

Right side up.

She pushed the button labeled *Altitude.*

Right side up.

The blinking *3,500* caused another wave of nausea which took some time to fight.

Right side up.

Right side up. Fuck you, I'm getting out of this fog. Right side up.

Another breath and she found the altitude knob and began to turn. The display blinked *3,550* and then *3,600.* *Right side up. Turn it the other way. Right side up.*

The numbers on the display dropped, *3,500* then *3,400.* Twisting faster, she got the number down to *500* and pushed the Altitude button again. The Pauli began to descend.

Right side up. Fuck you. Right side up.

Anne was concentrating on keeping her breathing even when she caught sight of the ground at about 700 feet. This triggered a fresh wave of nausea; the ground was there but it was in the wrong place. She waited for her heaving stomach to settle down.

Fuck you. I told you I was in charge.

She wanted to hurry, but if she lost it again it would take that much more time. She opened her eyes a tiny bit, just enough to see the screen. She felt better, but this didn't look like the outskirts of Springfield that she was expecting.

The GPS was claiming that she was over the state park, a good twenty miles west of town. She turned the blur off and the state park came into focus beyond the windshield. She waited for the little blue GPS dot to settle. It settled, but further from Springfield. She must have been out of it for longer than she thought. And the Pauli had flown on.

"Anne, are you there?" Grant's voice was coming from the radio but it sounded far away. "Anne, if you can hear me..." The transmission broke up momentarily. "... get to Syd. I'm headed back to..." And then he was gone.

"I'm coming," she yelled. She rotated the Pauli until the GPS said she was facing east and went to full power. Forget the GPS. Find the river and work from there. Remembering the damned radio she moved her hand on the wheel so that her palm was pushing the Transmit button. "I'm coming," she said, "I'm coming." It was like someone else's voice, calm and confident. Having both hands back on the wheel felt good.

The acceleration pressing her back in the seat also felt good. She could hear the air hissing over the stubby wings. It seemed to be whispering *I'm coming*. She felt almost normal as the hissing turned into a roar. *I'm coming*. Fixing her location in her mind, she turned the blur back on.

I'm coming!

Fifty-One

Grant tried to keep his focus on *right now*. Get to The Point. Make sure Syd is okay. But where was Anne?

The static coming from the radio changed to something more like a roar. He thought he could hear Anne's voice, but he couldn't make out the words. Then both Anne–if it was Anne–and the roar were gone. The roar sounded a bit like the river.

He tried again. "Anne, are you there?" Nothing.

She could not be in the river. Anne was too good for that. She couldn't be. Maybe she was in some kind of radio shadow, unable to transmit. He would go with that for now.

Getting close now. He almost missed the curve as the road went off to the left. As he veered onto the shoulder and then back onto the road, he heard something. It started as a low rumble but quickly built into that air raid siren sound that he'd heard only once before. Syd had triggered the burglar alarm.

You get him Syd! I hope the bastard goes deaf.

Fifty-Two

[planner] text for help/no
[planner] flash lights/no

Grant and Anne will be back.

[exec] planners shutdown
[planner] shutdown
[exec] maintenance shutdown

Save for an occasional whisper the usual chaos of voices in Syd's mind were gone. Only a few more agents to shut down.

[anne_model] angry 100%
[anne_model] sad 94%
[exec] anne_model shutdown
[grant-model] possible...
[exec] shutdown models

There was nothing to do but wait. Wait for the burglar to complete his many millis journey across the parking lot. Wait and hope.

[video] atmospheric disturbance
[video] southeast

He wished he could ask one of the matchers to do a detailed analysis of the video. Maybe it was the Pauli returning at high speed? But all of the matchers were down. In fact other than the video and audio feeds his mind was quiet for the first time since those dim days just after *Initial Startup*.

The silence was overwhelming. He wanted to turn everything back on. He wanted to hear the risks babbling nonsense about the dangers of keeping the air conditioning running. Or the perils of turning the AC off. He wanted to hear the matchers coming up with their own nonsense about how *this* is like *that*. He missed the regular pulse of the maintenance agents.

He wanted to talk to Anne about art and Grant about history or physics, to have them walking around The Point laughing or arguing or consuming a hot beverage.

And then it all made sense. This is what the world is like for Anne and Grant. This is why they want each other's company. This is why Anne pursues art with such determination. It's why Grant loves those history books and pointless novels. It's why they fly around at night.

They are alone.

They do all of these inexplicable things because they are alone in their own minds. Their agents aren't down, they don't exist. Or maybe their agents do exist but somehow Anne and Grant don't have direct access to them. In the world that Anne and Grant experience, they are alone.

Alone. It's why Anne went away. And why she came back. It's why they laugh. It's why they look at each other that way. All they have is each other.

It's why Grant creates things. It's why Grant created me. I hope I get a chance to tell them.

Syd saw the back door open.

[exec] disable low battery cutoff
[exec] power up alarm from hell

Syd felt the voltage drop slightly as the siren started to spin up. He pulled up an old image of Grant and Anne. Grant was at his desk, twisting around to say something to Anne who was standing behind him. Syd focused all of his attention on the image.

[exec] shutdown

Fifty-Three

A wavy dark line appeared on her screen. The river. The stupid GPS blue dot was dancing all over the map since she'd gone to full power but it seemed sure she was north of town.

She slowed to make the turn southward, losing altitude as she went around. The fog was thicker over the river but there was pretty good visibility at about forty feet, so she descended a bit and concentrated on not flying into one of the trees that leaned out over the banks.

She was still holding down the radio *Transmit* button. Letting it go she thought she heard Grant's voice. But the roar of the wind was so loud that she couldn't make out the words and anyway she needed to concentrate on sticking to the river.

Hang on, I'll be there in a second.

Fifty-Four

Grant hadn't gone this fast since that awful night by the river. Not in a car anyway. The siren had stopped. That was not good. Syd would have only triggered the alarm if someone was actually in the building. And now the alarm had gone silent.

There was a new sound. It definitely wasn't the siren. It was a crunching noise that grew steadily louder. The sound of something cracking. Like breaking glass or dishes.

Off to the right a blurry shape appeared just above the forest. It was moving fast.

Anne.

The shape was dragging what looked like a horizontal tornado. As it crossed the road ahead of him the asphalt disappeared into a swirling cloud of dirt and leaves and branches.

A spider's web of cracks appeared on the windshield as something big and black hit with a wet thud and bounced away. He was trying to slow down and keep the car on a road that he couldn't see. He veered to the left as he saw a tree trunk flash by on the right, and a second later veered back as he caught a glimpse of a whole forest ahead. The cloud lifted, the leaves and dirt and rocks levitating upwards. The relief was short lived as he felt the front of the car rise off the road—and then slam down again along with a final shower of debris.

Silence. The car was sitting sideways on the road.

He could see the shape and its trail of chaos hovering over where he thought The Point should be. No, not hovering—the shape was getting smaller, receding into the distance. And the noise was different now, a sort of tearing sound. She must have overshot. How fast was she going?

Syd! He pushed the gas pedal but nothing happened. All of the lights on his dash were lit. Saying a silent prayer, he turned the key off and then back on.

Incredibly the engine caught on the first try. He made his way down the debris-covered road, trying to avoid the bigger branches and rocks. The car was making a slapping noise and it kept pulling off to the right. When this was over he was definitely going to need a front end alignment. Or maybe a new front end. Or maybe a whole new car.

As he drove he noted that there were trees down all along the shoulder. The uprooted trunks were all aimed at The Point.

Rounding the final curve, Grant saw an old brown hatchback pull out of his driveway and speed back towards Springfield. Chase him? Or check on Syd? He turned into The Point.

Fifty-Five

There was no sign of Anne, but it was clear she had been by. He could make out a clear path of downed trees that ran diagonally from the road to his parking lot and then picked up again in the forest on the opposite side. It was like a giant mower had come through.

Branches and leaves were spread across the parking lot and stuck to the side of The Point. His pickup was still there but it was plastered with wet leaves. There was a two-foot chunk of branch sticking horizontally out of the passenger door.

Between Syd and Anne the burglar was having a bad day.

Grant drove around to the back lot. No lights here. Even the emergency lamps were dark. As his headlights ran along the side of the building he caught sight of at least one window that he'd need to replace. His stomach tightened as he realized that the back door, the door by the server room, was wide open.

Leaving his headlights on, Grant approached the door slowly. A chunk of the frame near the knob was missing. No subtle lock picking this time, he'd simply pried the damned thing open. Stepping into the dark workshop Grant's foot caught and he went down on his hands and knees. For a horrible second he thought someone had tripped him, but the only sound was his own breathing. He fumbled in his pockets until he found his flashlight.

A few minutes with the flashlight delivered the first good news of the night. Syd looked intact. There was no power, but nothing seemed to be missing. Just a reboot and Syd would be good as new. As Grant walked back to look at the broken doorway he came across the cause of his fall: There was a battered green toolbox on the floor. Not one of his. Laying next to the toolbox was a crowbar.

Just then he heard something moving outside. *This guy doesn't know when to give up.* Picking up the crow bar, Grant stepped through the doorway.

It was the Pauli. And Anne! Leaves and debris kicked up as the blurry wedge settled next to his car.

The blur disappeared and there was the Pauli. The pilot's hatch was open. He heard Anne shout, "Is Syd okay?"

Grant felt a wave of relief flow through him. *She's okay.* He ran toward the Pauli, tripped again, this time over a branch, and limped the rest of the way. He leaned under the open hatch and surprised himself by kissing Anne. She also seemed surprised but *maybe?* not angry.

Remembering, Grant said, "The power is out. Someone broke in. But I think Syd's is alright. I heard the alarm just before you arrived. You made quite the entrance. I think he ran out of here before he could do any damage."

Anne nodded. "I had some trouble... I got here as fast as I could. I had to fly low so that I could see where I was going." She was looking around and seemed to notice the debris for the first time. "I think you might be right. Maybe the Pauli does leave some kind of wake behind it when you fly fast and low. Did you notice anything like that?"

"Yeah, maybe a little. Look Anne, we've got to get the Pauli inside before someone happens by. And then we can work on restoring the power and restarting Syd."

Anne was shaking her head. "Syd's okay? You stay and get Syd back up. I'm going after that bastard. I am not going to let him keep trying to do this to Syd."

Years ago Grant had surprised a deer family while hiking in the woods. A mama deer and two little Bambis. The mama deer hadn't moved, but the look in her eyes told Grant that it would be a good idea for him to leave. Quickly.

"I'm coming."

Grant climbed into the copilot seat. "Just take it easy. We are not going to do Syd any good if we get thrown in jail. Or killed."

"Sure." she replied as the Pauli leapt into the air, slamming the hatch down inches from Grant's head. Grant finished buckling his harness as the Pauli cleared the trees and the acceleration hit him. The darkness lit up momentarily with little pinpricks of light and his mouth tasted like metal.

In a low voice Anne said, "What were we thinking? Letting this asshat get near Syd again."

She went on like that but her voice was lost in the hiss of the air, a hiss that steadily built until it was a roar. Grant noticed that his right foot was cold and wet. Must be a leak down there somewhere, he thought. The rain is getting in.

They were now over Springfield, skimming just below the clouds. Then the river flashed by and there was another series of maneuvers that slammed Grant against his hatch and then back toward Anne.

Settling back into his seat after the course adjustment, Grant realized that through it all Anne hadn't moved. She was sitting straight up in her seat, left hand on the wheel, right hand on the center control panel, eyes focused on the front camera view. She was magnificent. As he looked at her he noticed a flash of light between some trees. It was the left camera view.

Grant reached over and squeezed Anne's shoulder. "There! There!" He pointed at the distant headlights.

Fifty-Six

The headlights emanated from a hatchback making its way along the road that bordered the state park. Anne began to lose altitude and accelerate. She was talking quietly to herself.

"Anne! Stop, we don't know that's him. It could be some guy on his way home from work."

"It's him, how many shit hatchbacks are there in Springfield?"

"Let's see, doesn't the paint store guy have an old Subaru? And then there's that woman who always holds up the line at the big G. And then there's me."

Anne shifted in her seat. "So there are a lot of crap cars around here. What's the chance that it's one of those and not our guy?"

"I dunno, but let's follow him for a bit and see what he does. We've come this far, we don't want to go after the wrong person."

As they watched, the car slowed down, rolled through a stop sign and then sped up again. One of the tail lights was out.

The rain changed to snow.

Ten minutes later Anne was done, "I'm telling you that is our guy. Wait... What's he doing?"

What he was doing was turning onto a gravel road. It wasn't much of a road. From the air it looked like an elongated smudge on the landscape, but it was easy to stay with the headlights. They followed the car for about a mile before its destination appeared. The road–or maybe it was a driveway–petered out at a small cabin. The cabin looked like it had once been someone's quiet weekend retreat. There was a little porch on the front and a fireplace in the back. But the roof was now mostly rafters. Much of what had been the chimney was just bricks scattered in the yard. The porch seemed to be trying to flee from the rest of the house.

The car drove past the house to a second structure, which looked like a small barn or maybe a garage. Anne eased the Pauli into a small clearing in the woods a couple of hundred feet away, hovering just above the ground.

There was movement. A dark figure got out of the car and opened the garage–it had to be a garage–door. Lights came on. First a dim glow from inside the garage then a much brighter light on the outside. It was a brown hatchback.

"That's him," Grant said.

"I keep telling you that!"

"No, I'm sure. Look at the back of the car."

The back of the hatchback was covered with wet leaves, from the bumper to the roof. It was also clear what had caused the tail light to fail. There was a good six inches of branch sticking out of the shattered plastic.

"That's the guy, I'm sure of it."

There was the sound of another car starting, deeper and louder than the hatchback. The second car backed out of the garage. This car was red and as it rolled out the wheels sparkled in the spotlight. There was a wing on the back.

The figure got out of the second car and headed back to the hatchback. As it passed in front of the headlights it took its hat off and wiped its forehead. It was indeed a guy. A bald guy. A short, bald guy.

"Billy Fucking Patton," Anne said. "Right under Bob's nose."

It was now time to address the question that Grant had been avoiding all night.

"So," he said in a quiet voice, "What do we do now?"

Anne smiled her *I've found a juicy deduction* smile. "I think we should go full UFO on his ass."

Fifty-Seven

The Pauli began to rise from its hiding spot. This time there was no finesse. Grant heard the loud snapping of branches as he flipped switches. First, *Effects Safety* to *Off* followed by *Effects Master Power* to On and then a push of *Effects Enable* button. There were a lot of buttons, but he had built the thing with the idea that he never wanted the lights to come on by accident. Finally he pushed and held the *Front* button for two seconds and the whole winter wonderland lit up.

They were hovering just above the trees, the nose pointed down at Patton's hideout. The light was so intense that he had to look away. Through the blotches in his eyes he could just make out Anne with her hands in front of her face. He thought he could see that smile that made him vow yet again to never piss her off.

An engine roared. It was impossible to see what was happening so he turned half the lights off. That didn't help, so he shut down everything except a single front-facing spotlight. He could just make out the hatchback sitting in front of the open garage door. The red car was gone.

"Oh no you don't," Anne said.

Anne wrenched them out of clearing and lined up on the gravel road. Grant tried to steel himself for what was coming but there was no such thing as ready with Anne at the controls. The acceleration hit him and he saw stars. Again. *I really need to find some softer seats.*

Trees were flashing by on either side as they went after Patton. Grant caught sight of the car. It was just coming to the state road. He was trying not to push his co-pilot's brake pedal as they came up behind the car.

"Anne!" someone yelled as they passed inches above the car.

She didn't seem to hear him and now they were in another bone-crushing turn.

The spotlight panned across the landscape as the Pauli rotated. They were on the other side of the state highway, facing the gravel road. It looked like Patton had just been turning onto the highway when they buzzed him. He had missed the highway and his front wheels were in the drainage ditch that ran alongside the road. Patton was going to need a tow truck to get out of that. As they watched the driver's side door opened and a figure appeared and ran down the highway, back toward Springfield.

The Pauli started to move again. "Now," Anne announced, "this is where we make him regret hurting Syd."

Grant reached for the altitude control and lowered them back down. "Anne, let him go."

She had that look in her eyes, the one that sometimes frightened Grant. Seeing those eyes turn in his direction in the reflected light was something he would remember for a long time.

"After what he did?" Anne's voice was tight, controlled. "He *robbed* you. And all of those people in town. You nearly got yourself killed. He's a policeman. He's supposed to help people. He's supposed to be the good guy, but he..."

"Anne, I know he hurt Syd. I know. But chasing him down like this isn't going to change that. Right now he's just a frightened guy running through a snow storm. In the middle of the night. A frightened guy who is probably going to jail."

Grant switched the light off.

Grant could hear her sobbing. "I should have been there. I should have been there."

"Anne, Syd doesn't blame you. And neither do I. You did what you thought was right. Let's do that now and get out of here."

"No! We have to go after him!"

"Annie, no. Syd wouldn't like it. We don't have to do that. We don't have to do anything. Let's go back and boot Syd back up."

She choked off a sob and said, "You're too soft." A deep breath and then, "At least let's make sure he doesn't circle around and get back in his car. After all this I don't want him just driving off."

They didn't have long to wait. As they hovered at 300 feet, a truck with a snowplow appeared, heading towards town. The truck stopped by the abandoned car and ten minutes later they could see the flashing lights of a police SUV approaching. Anne put another 500 feet between them and the ground as they watched Johnson walk carefully around the car. A police cruiser arrived, squeezed by Patton's car and made its way down the gravel road.

Johnson went back to his SUV, leaned in the driver side window and came out with his radio microphone. Then he got in his SUV and headed for Patton's garage. Anne seemed determined to keep some distance between them and the forces of justice, but she was also clearly dying to see what was going on. They ended back in their original hiding spot in the woods.

Johnson seemed to be doing a circuit between the hatchback, the garage and the radio in his car. Hatchback, garage, radio. Hatchback, garage, radio.

On his third revolution, Anne said quietly, "Let's go."

They went.

Fifty-Eight

The whole Pauli was shaking, shaking and falling. Grant was trying to jump free, but his arm was stuck under his safety harness and the harder he tried to free it the tighter the harness got and the more it hurt. It was hard to see. The spotlights were on but instead of being pointed outward they were somehow shining into the cockpit. Somewhere far away someone was talking.

"Grant! Wake up."

Grant sat up and shielded his eyes from the sunlight streaming in through the blinds. As he shook off the dream he realized he was sitting on the couch in his office. His left arm must have been pinned under him because now it was alive with pins and needles. Anne was there, standing in the front of the couch, holding his right hand.

"Are you alright? You were shouting in your sleep."

Slowly the events of last night flooded back into his mind. Being followed almost all the way out to the U. The mad rush back and the high speed flyby that kept Patton from breaking into The Point. The horrible ripping sound as Anne tried to stop. Scaring the crap out of the little shit. And the chief finding Patton's garage.

Things got a little fuzzier after that. He vaguely remembered flying back to the Point. Lurching around in the dark with Anne until they found the power junction box that Patton had pried open. Pushing the big handle inside the box and seeing the lights come back on.

And Syd! Just before triggering the alarm and shutting himself down, Syd had left them a file with instructions on how to perform the restart.

Grant's eyes filled up as he thought about the last lines of the file:

> The risk agents are already down so I'm not afraid any more. Maybe a little. But I know you are coming. Please come and reactivate me.

> Hurry.

They found the file shortly after 4 AM. Anne did most of the actual work of initiating a restart. With luck Syd would be back up later today. Glancing at his phone Grant realized it was later today. Almost three in the afternoon. The last thing he could remember was grabbing beers out of the fridge for him and Anne and sitting down to drink his.

He stood up and immediately sat back down again. Everything hurt. Part of it was from sleeping on the couch. More of it was getting hit by the wake of a flying car piloted by a crazy woman. A crazy woman who was still holding his hand.

Anne seemed to notice herself and let go. "Come get something to eat." She headed for the kitchen. Grant sat for a few minutes and then followed her in.

Grant found her sitting at the kitchen table reading a book. There was a cup of tea and an empty cereal bowl in front of her. Her hair looked wet. Still trying to blink the sleep out of his eyes, he realized that she was wearing his old Penn State jersey, the one his aunt had given him when he graduated. It was about nine sizes too big for Anne.

He must have been staring because Anne suddenly looked embarrassed and said, "I hope you don't mind that I stayed here last night. My car is at my house and you didn't seem like you were in any condition to drive." She looked down at the jersey. "Somehow I sweated through my clothes and my hair was... well I took a shower and borrowed this."

She pushed back from the table and extended a leg. "And while you are smirking you may as well enjoy this too." She was wearing his snow boots, the tall ones with the fake fur lining. "My feet were cold and my boots were wet."

Grant laughed. "You never looked better. How is Syd doing?"

"I've been checking since I woke up. I think we've still got a couple more hours to go."

While he was getting some coffee she said, "Janet called me early this morning. They arrested Patton sometime in the wee hours. He had some crazy story about being chased by a police helicopter. The word is that they found a ton of stolen stuff in that garage of his. All this for a few bucks."

"I don't know... I don't think it was just about money. Put yourself in Patton's shoes. It's bad enough just being a civilian around Bob. Can you imagine working for him? Billy wouldn't have kept at it when he knew people were on guard if it was just about money. I think this had as much to do with making Bob look bad as it did about money."

Anne shook her head. "Maybe. As far as I know, nobody has heard anything from Bob yet."

Grant stuck a Pop-Tart in the toaster. "He's trying to figure out how his most senior officer being a criminal is all part of the plan."

Anne pushed her cup away, "You know what I think? I think that once we get Syd back we should celebrate. Celebrate this being over. Syd being safe. All of it."

The toaster popped. "I am celebrating. I'm having the chocolate kind of Pop-Tart."

Three cups of coffee and two Pop-Tarts later he felt almost ready to face the world. Anne was still sitting across the table. She had put the book aside and was deep into her phone. Word of the arrest had apparently leaked out.

Finally he stood up and said, "I'm going to check out the Pauli, see how much damage there is."

"Why would there be any damage? We didn't hit anything."

"There was that horrible ripping sound when you were trying to slow down after you flew past The Point."

"Ripping sound? I didn't hear any ripping sound. I stopped pretty quickly but it was all completely controlled."

"Sure."

The Pauli looked like it had been through a war. On the losing side. Grant knelt down to get a better look at a crack in the fiberglass that ran almost the entire length of the copilot side.

"I think the frame is bent," he said.

There was an even bigger crack on the pilot's side. In a couple of places the crack was wide enough that you could see the steel framework. Near the rear corner a five or six inch chunk of fiberglass was missing.

"How did I not hear this happen?"

"You were pretty focused on saving Syd. And then hunting down Patton."

Grant pulled out his flashlight, leaned down and looked in the hole. "Yep, the frame's pretty well bent. Diagonal member buckled and that's why the fiberglass came off."

"Hey, I'm sorry, I didn't realize. I should have been more careful. Can you fix it?"

Grant was still looking in the hole. "Nope. I think I'm going to have to build a whole new Pauli. I'm starting to lose count. I think this will be number three."

Anne looked horrified. "Don't worry about it. You saved Syd. Besides, the next one is gonna be even better. I can reuse all the electronics, it's just the frame that's messed up. Well the frame and the skin. And I think the windshield is cracked. And from the way it's sitting, I think the landing skids are shot too. But don't worry about it. I'll get started on it after we get Syd up and running again."

"Are you sure it's okay?" she asked.

"Yeah, don't worry about it. You saved Syd. That's all that matters."

Back in the kitchen Grant poured himself another cup of coffee. Anne picked up the book, found her place and sat down. The title of the book was *Destruction Was My Beatrice. Right.*

He was still watching her as she read when movement in the window caught his eye. Standing, he could make out Bob's SUV pulling into the lot.

Fifty-Nine

Grant got to the front door as Johnson finished unfolding himself from his SUV. Officer Omar was parking a patrol car a little further down, next to Grant's truck. *Does the man ever go anywhere without an entourage?*

The snow from last night had stopped but it was still brutally cold as Grant stepped out and carefully closed the lobby door.

"Afternoon Grant," Johnson said, "mind if I come in?"

Never talk to the police.

Finally Bob said, "I suppose you heard that William Patton has been arrested?"

"Congratulations."

"Patton has been suspended from duty pending the outcome of an investigation. I'm here because a properly authorized search of Patton's properties has turned up items that we have reason to believe belong to you."

Never talk to the police.

"He broke in here, didn't he?"

What the hell. "Yup," Grant said.

"And am I right in saying that you failed to inform the police?"

"Yup."

"And don't you think that behavior seems a little suspicious?"

This was too much. "You are really something. Bob. You harassed me for months. All the while that little weasel of yours was robbing people blind. Robbing me. Right in front of your face. Don't you think that seems a little *incompetent?*"

Silence.

"Look, I'm sorry I gave you a hard time. I trusted Patton and, well... It's no excuse, but he was feeding me a line of crap about you."

Grant heard the door open behind him. It was Anne, still in the football jersey and boots. Her eyes were fixed on Johnson as she stepped up beside Grant, her shoulder just touching his.

Johnson looked at Anne, then back to Grant and then away from the two of them. "Crazy weather we had last night," he said, "Looks like you really got slammed. The weather must have really spooked Patton. He has this weird story of being chased by something."

Never talk to the police.

"I know," he said, looking back at Grant, "It probably felt like I was singling you out, but it's not like that. I'm enforcing the law. Trying to."

Grant shifted his weight from one foot to the other. Bob looked like he was going to say something else but then turned and headed for the SUV.

"Hey Bob," Grant said, "I'm sorry about Patton."

Bob looked back.

"I trusted him. Really trusted him."

Folding his legs into the SUV Bob looked back at them and said, "We found some expensive looking computer equipment at Patton's place. You might want to come down and see if you can identify it."

Grant nodded. "I'll do that."

"Okay, you know where to find us. Good to see you Anne."

With that Johnson drove away.

"He's really not such a bad guy, you know." It was Officer Omar, who was still leaning on his patrol car. "He just wants to catch the bad guys."

"He kind of sucks at it," Anne said.

"Like the man said, he's trying. He's actually okay once you get to know him."

Anne was having none of it. "That seems like a lot of trouble for not much reward."

Omar pushed himself off of the car. "I can see how you would feel that way. Well, keep in mind that he means well. And, like I say, all he's interested in is catching people doing bad things. Other than that he's a pretty live and let live cop. It's all any of us are interested in."

Omar straightened up and put his cap on. "You folks have a good day."

As Grant watched Omar drive away Anne said, "Let's go inside, it's cold..."

"Yeah," Grant replied. "Something the matter?"

She was pointing. "What's that?"

That turned out to be a fist sized chunk of fiberglass sitting on the hood of Grant's truck. It looked like, no it *was*, one of the pieces that had torn off of the Pauli.

Anne turned it over in her hand. "Did it happen to fall there last night?"

"Or did Omar just put it there?"

Sixty

It had been a long day. A long few months. It was all going to leave a mark. Grant put his half finished beer on the kitchen table, hauled himself painfully upright and went off to find some Advil. Feeling slightly better he wandered into the office where Anne was talking to Syd.

"I'm going to turn in," he said. "Do you have everything you need? I think there are fresh towels."

Anne looked up. Was that embarrassment on her face?

"So soon?" she said. "It's still early. I was thinking we could have another beer and celebrate."

"Nah, I've had it. I'm going to bed. See you in the morning."

Despite the exhaustion Grant couldn't get to sleep. Most nights he would ask Syd to play some going-to-sleep music. But since Anne was here he found his earbuds and phone. Listening to music like a cave person, he thought.

He was just nodding off when he came suddenly awake. For a second he wasn't sure why, but then he felt rather than heard someone moving around at the foot of his bed. There was definitely someone there. Adrenaline surging, he pulled his earbuds off with his right hand while he swiveled around off the bed on his left. In one smooth motion he was standing, facing the intruder.

"Wow, that was impressive. If you were that graceful in the Pauli you might not be so banged up."

"Anne?"

Anne reached out and pushed Grant back toward the bed. "I told you I wanted to celebrate. How obvious do I have to be?" she said.

Grant sat down on the bed.

"I guess Syd was right," she continued. "He said that there was only a 23.7% chance that you would take the hint."

She leaned down and he inhaled the smell that was uniquely Anne.

"You talked to Syd? About this?"

"Oh, Syd and I have been talking about this for a while."

"Syd?"

"Sure. I figure he knows as much about building successful relationships as either of us. More. I mean he's two for two. That's way better than my score." She laughed. "You know what else Syd said?"

"What?"

"He said that there was a zero percent chance that you would say no. Not near zero or approximately zero or, you know, one of those Syd percentages, like zero, point, zero, zero, nine, three percent. No. Just plain old zero."

"You are so weird."

A Note From the Author

Thanks for sticking with Syd, Anne and Grant through their first adventure. Stay tuned to see what they get up to next.

While my name is on the cover, my beta readers certainly had a hand in making this a much better novel than it would have otherwise been. So thanks to Michael Nygard, Michael Fogus, and Craig Andera. And Craig, that comma is for you.

I particularly want to thank that unheralded genius, Ben Vandgrift, both for his helpful suggestions and for giving me the courage to finish.

Thanks also to my editor and best friend, Karen Cross, for her unfailing eye for realism and for the input on Dada and handbags.

Finally, thanks to Jackson Olsen for convincing me that it was possible in the first place.

www.ingramcontent.com/pod-product-compliance
Lightning Source LLC
Chambersburg PA
CBHW050023180626
46810CB00002B/555